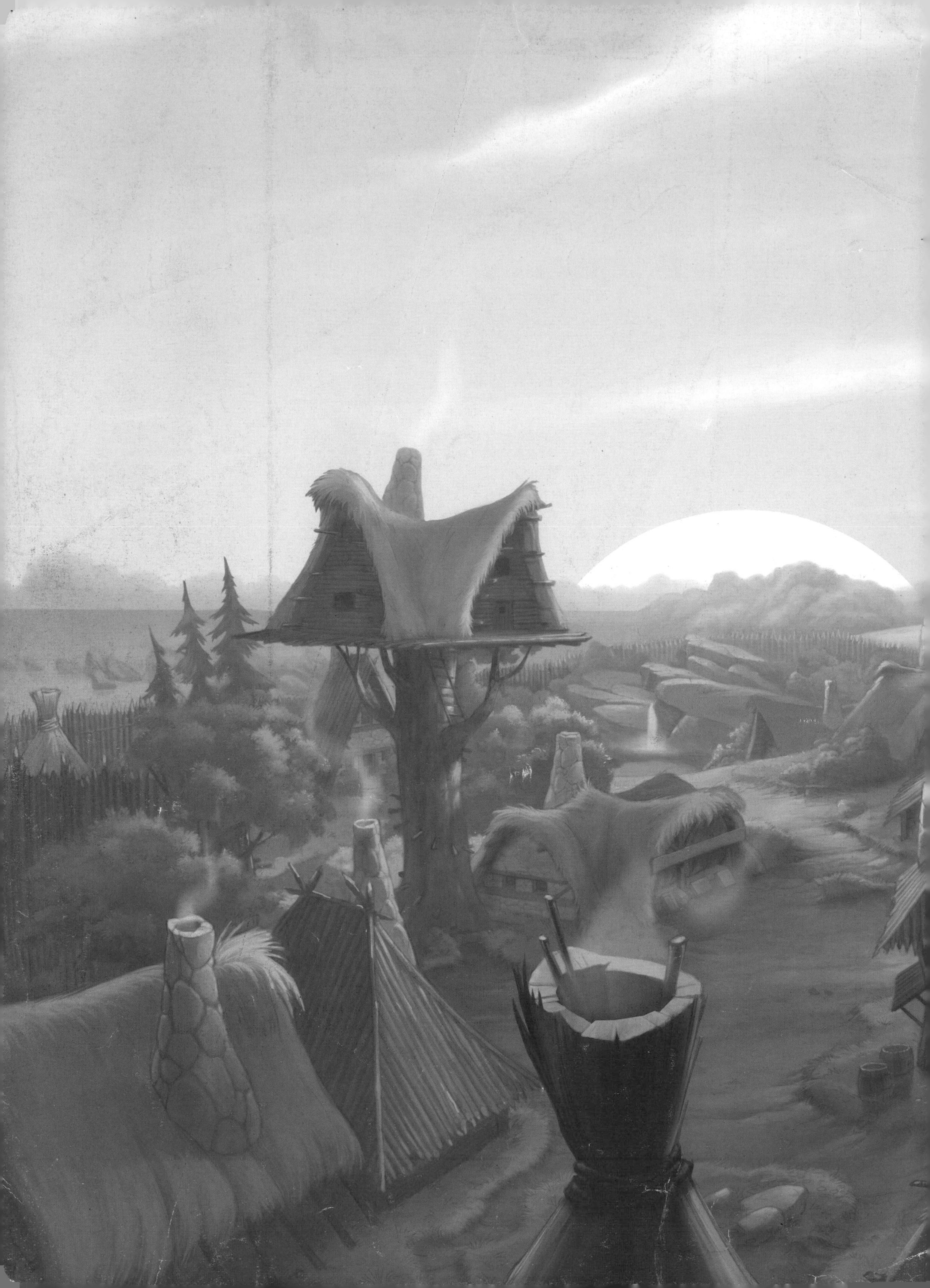

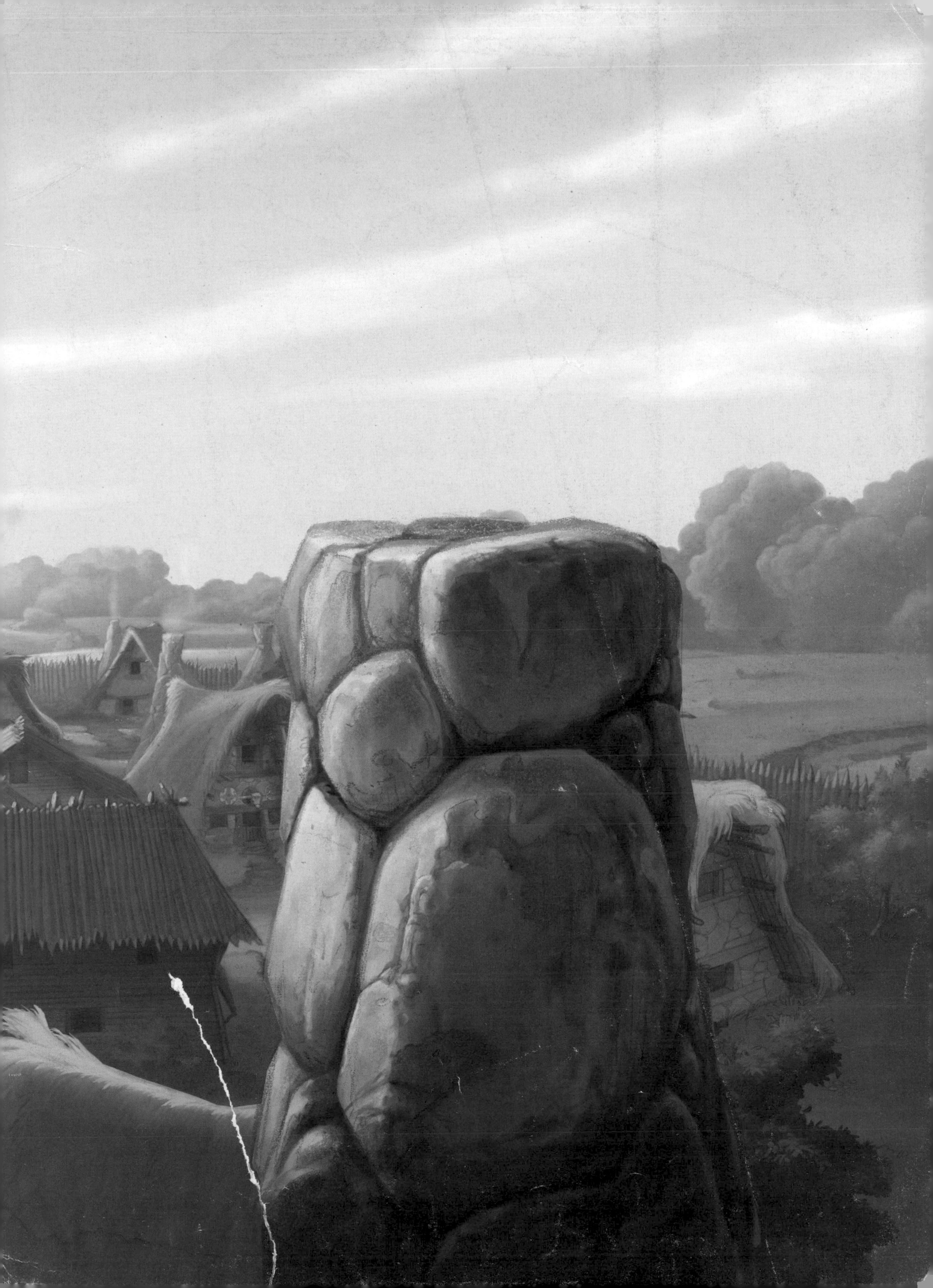

ORION CHILDREN'S BOOKS

This album is a tie-in to the animated film *Asterix and the Vikings*,
an M6 Studio production – Mandarin SAS – 2d3D Animations,
based on the album *Asterix and the Normans*
by René Goscinny and Albert Uderzo (Orion Books)

Film produced by **Stefan Fjeldmark** and **Jesper Møller**
Screenplay and screenwriting: **Jean-Luc Goossens**
In collaboration with **Stefan Fjeldmark**
Additional screenwriting: **Philip Lazebnik**

Asterix and the Vikings: © 2006 – M6 Studio – Mandarin SAS – 2d3D Animations
Adaptation rights: Les Éditions Albert René

ASTERIX®-OBELIX®
Original title: *Astérix et les Vikings*

Original edition © 2006 Les Éditions Albert René/Goscinny-Uderzo
English translation © 2006 Les Éditions Albert René/Goscinny-Uderzo

All adaptation and translation rights for any country reserved by Les Éditions Albert René

Exclusive Licensee: Hachette Children's Group
Translator: Anthea Bell
Typography: Bryony Newhouse

3 5 7 9 10 8 6 4 2

A CIP catalogue record for this book is available from the British Library.

ISBN: 978 0 7528 8590 2 HARDBACK
ISBN: 978 0 7528 8876 7 TRADE PAPERBACK
ISBN: 978 1 4440 1342 9 EBOOK

Printed in China
The paper and board used in this book are from well-managed forests and other responsible sources.

Orion Children's Books
An imprint of Hachette Children's Group, part of Hodder and Stoughton
Carmelite House, 50 Victoria Embankment
London EC4Y 0DZ
An Hachette UK Company

www.hachette.co.uk
www.asterix.com
www.hachettechildrens.co.uk

GOSCINNY AND UDERZO
PRESENT

Asterix® and the VIKINGS

THE BOOK OF THE FILM

Editorial concept: BB2C Conseil
Collaboration on the text: Marlène Soreda
Collaboration on the design: Studio 56

Translated by Anthea Bell

Orion
Children's Books

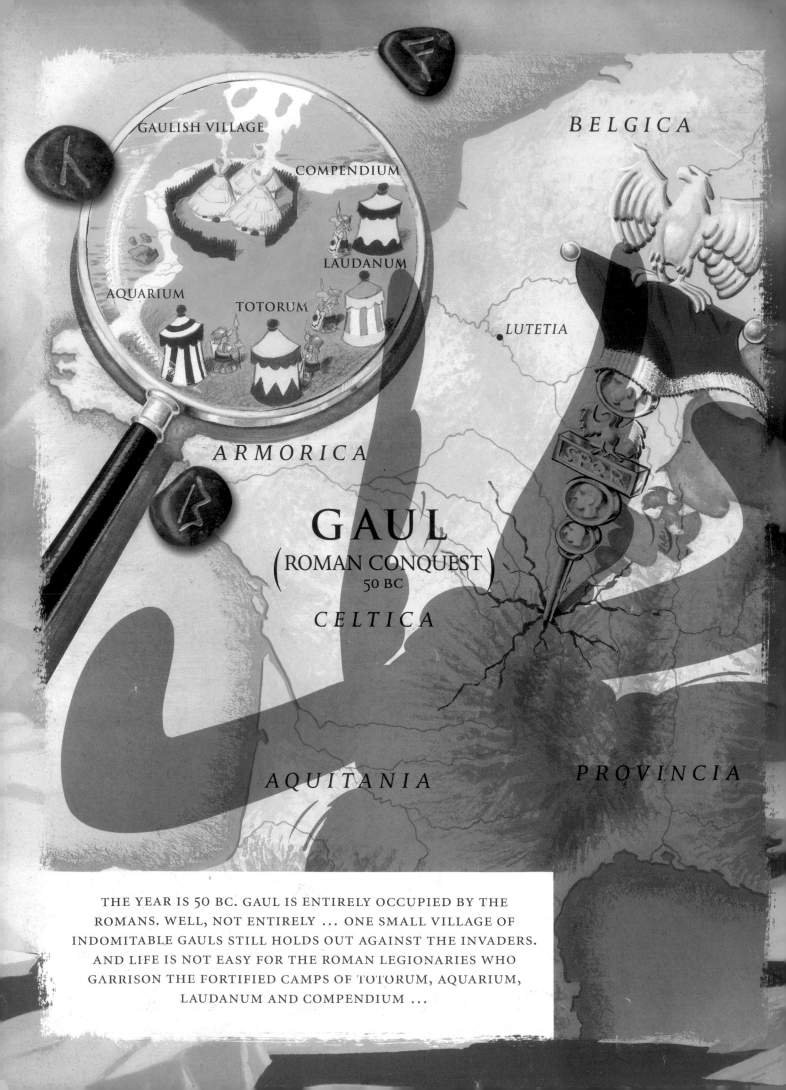

GAULISH VILLAGE

COMPENDIUM

LAUDANUM

AQUARIUM

TOTORUM

BELGICA

LUTETIA

ARMORICA

GAUL
(ROMAN CONQUEST)
50 BC

CELTICA

AQUITANIA

PROVINCIA

THE YEAR IS 50 BC. GAUL IS ENTIRELY OCCUPIED BY THE
ROMANS. WELL, NOT ENTIRELY ... ONE SMALL VILLAGE OF
INDOMITABLE GAULS STILL HOLDS OUT AGAINST THE INVADERS.
AND LIFE IS NOT EASY FOR THE ROMAN LEGIONARIES WHO
GARRISON THE FORTIFIED CAMPS OF TOTORUM, AQUARIUM,
LAUDANUM AND COMPENDIUM ...

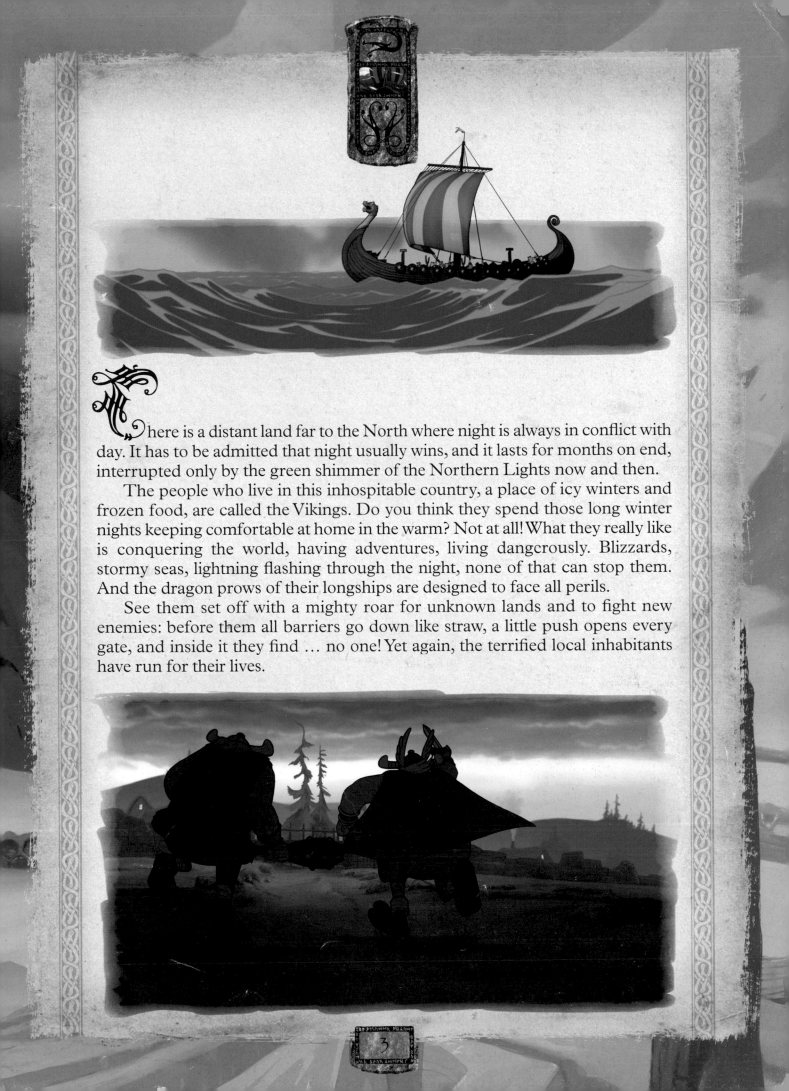

There is a distant land far to the North where night is always in conflict with day. It has to be admitted that night usually wins, and it lasts for months on end, interrupted only by the green shimmer of the Northern Lights now and then.

The people who live in this inhospitable country, a place of icy winters and frozen food, are called the Vikings. Do you think they spend those long winter nights keeping comfortable at home in the warm? Not at all! What they really like is conquering the world, having adventures, living dangerously. Blizzards, stormy seas, lightning flashing through the night, none of that can stop them. And the dragon prows of their longships are designed to face all perils.

See them set off with a mighty roar for unknown lands and to fight new enemies: before them all barriers go down like straw, a little push opens every gate, and inside it they find … no one! Yet again, the terrified local inhabitants have run for their lives.

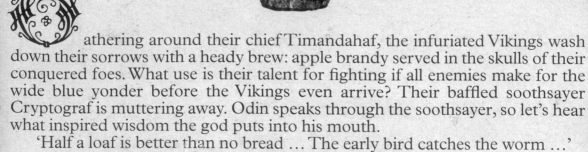

athering around their chief Timandahaf, the infuriated Vikings wash down their sorrows with a heady brew: apple brandy served in the skulls of their conquered foes. What use is their talent for fighting if all enemies make for the wide blue yonder before the Vikings even arrive? Their baffled soothsayer Cryptograf is muttering away. Odin speaks through the soothsayer, so let's hear what inspired wisdom the god puts into his mouth.

'Half a loaf is better than no bread … The early bird catches the worm …'

This is sending Timandahaf to sleep. The soothsayer is just droning on. Nothing he says explains why their enemies are so elusive. Cryptograf carries on translating the divine message into its VV.*

'Odin teaches … that fear lends you wings …'

'By Odin! By Thor! By gum!' The chief is cooking up a brainstorm under his helmet. 'Fear lends you wings? That's the answer! Let's learn the meaning of fear and then we'll know how to fly too! What we need is a coward, a scaredy-cat, a lily-livered poltroon! Let's go and find one and then, now that we've conquered the earth and the sea, the sky itself will be ours too!'

The Vikings are famous for their wide experience and fine navigation, and their name itself tells you how adventurous they are,** but nobody's perfect: they don't know what a figure of speech is. Listen to them shouting in unison, repeating their chief's words.

'We want fear! We want wings!'

Timandahaf is staking his all on this adventure: he promises to give the man who can capture a champion of the art of fear anything he asks.

'Anything? Do you really mean it?' The crafty Cryptograf is laughing up his sleeve.

'Yes, anything! But first tell us where we can find this rare being! Which way do we sail the longships?'

A look of evil calculation comes into the soothsayer's eyes. See him unfurl a rolled-up map and cast the fateful runes. It's like gambling in a casino … No more bets, the die is cast … no, ladies and gentlemen, no more bets taken at all now. And the rune Fehu, the sign of abundance, lands on a certain point on the coast of Armorica.

*Viking version.   **To go 'viking' meant to go on an adventure.

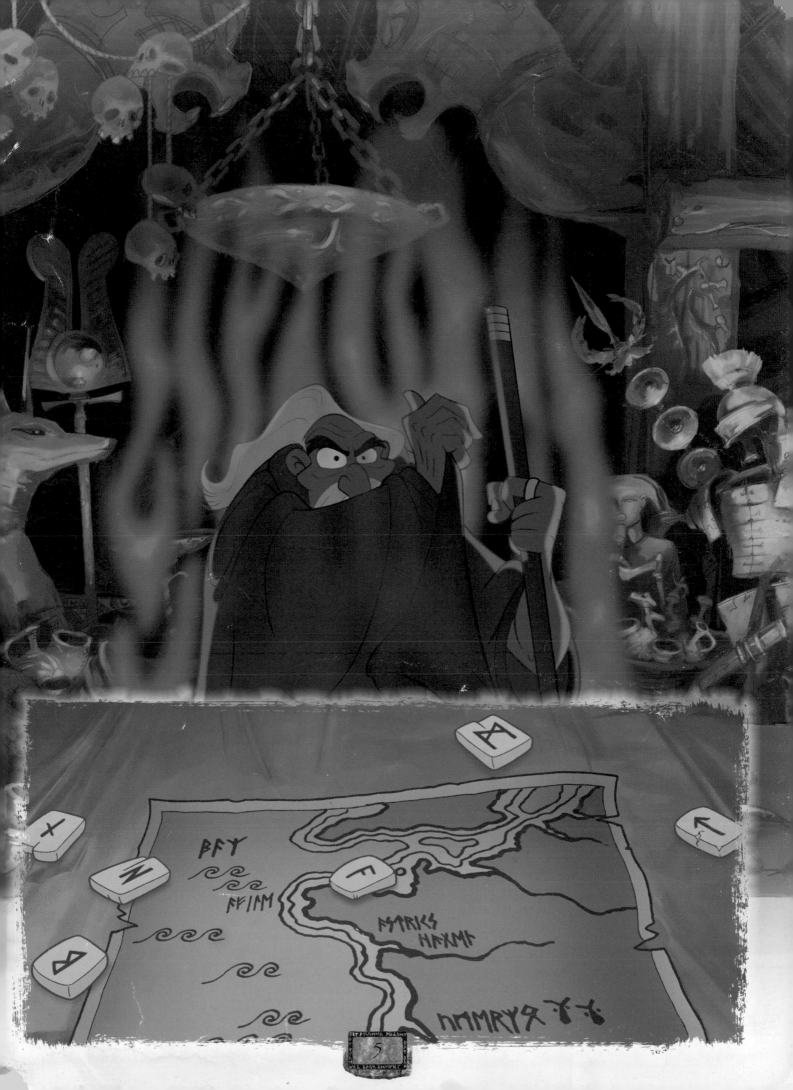

In fact it lands in that peaceful, happy village where the Gauls are indulging in one of their favourite pastimes: a lively debate about fish, fresh or otherwise. Asterix and Obelix are off to join the happy fray when Chief Vitalstatistix and his shield-bearers arrive. The village chieftain has just had a letter from Lutetia. It's from his brother Doublehelix, and the news in it concerns the whole village. Doublehelix, famous for fighting beside Vercingetorix at the battle of Gergovia, is sending his son Justforkix to stay with his uncle in the country. He feels that city life has left the teenager rather too soft. Vitalstatistix decides that it will be up to Asterix and Obelix to make a man of him, while the entire village will prepare a welcoming banquet.

Meanwhile, the fish fight goes on.

But suddenly the fish stop flying, and all heads turn to look at the young man driving up in his showy chariot, his long blond hair flying in the wind as his two horses gallop full speed ahead. Spreading panic among the chickens, the chariot and pair comes to a halt in the middle of the village with a fairly well-controlled skid. Vitalstatistix, slightly surprised by his nephew's spectacular arrival, is starting to introduce everyone when a dove flies down to join the young man.

'Meet SMS,' he explains to the Gauls. 'She provides my short-message service.'

Before the eyes of the startled villagers the dove, vibrating convulsively, pecks out her message on a wooden post with the speed and precision of a woodpecker. Rather disappointed to find his hosts so technologically backward, Justforkix asks what's for supper. 'Your fish doesn't look very fresh.'

This tactless remark takes instant effect: the fish fight hadn't gone on nearly long enough, and now it can resume.

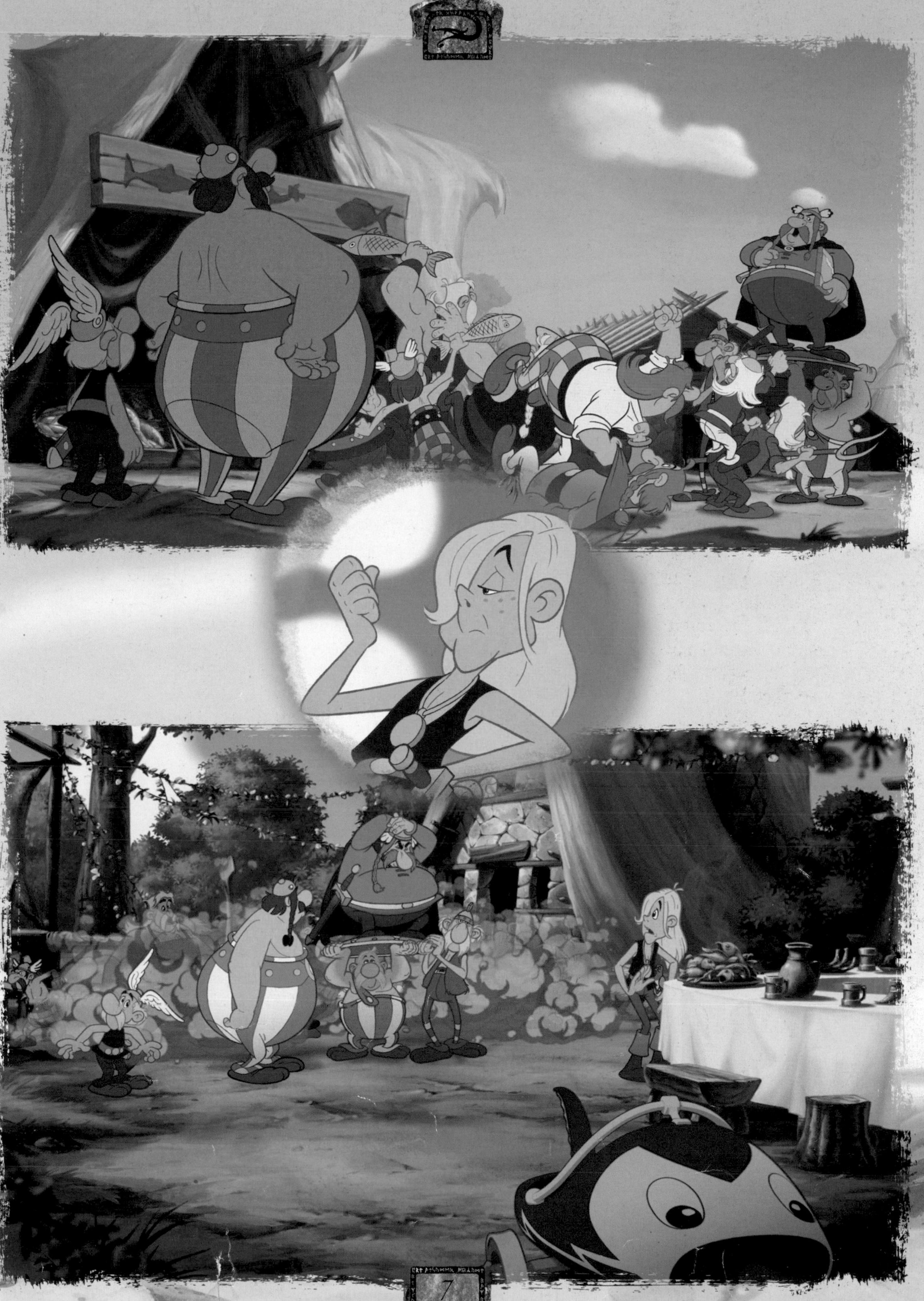

When night falls, spits are turning, wild boar are roasting, and everyone is keen to get to know the young man. City ways meet country life: all the girls and young women want to hear about the bright lights and nightclubs of Lutetia. To Obelix's horror, Justforkix turns out to be a vegetarian. Obelix earnestly tries to convince him of the nutritional value of wild boar.

Time for the dancing to begin! A row of women faces a row of men; they take a few steps forward, a few steps back, then to one side … Bored out of his mind, Justforkix won't join in. This is stuff for the golden oldies!

'How do they dance in Lutetia?' Impedimenta asks.

'Hey, why don't I show you?' And the hip young man jumps up on the platform, pushing the bard aside and gyrating wildly in trendy modern style. He looks as if he's dislocating all his joints. The catchy rhythm gradually takes the villagers over.

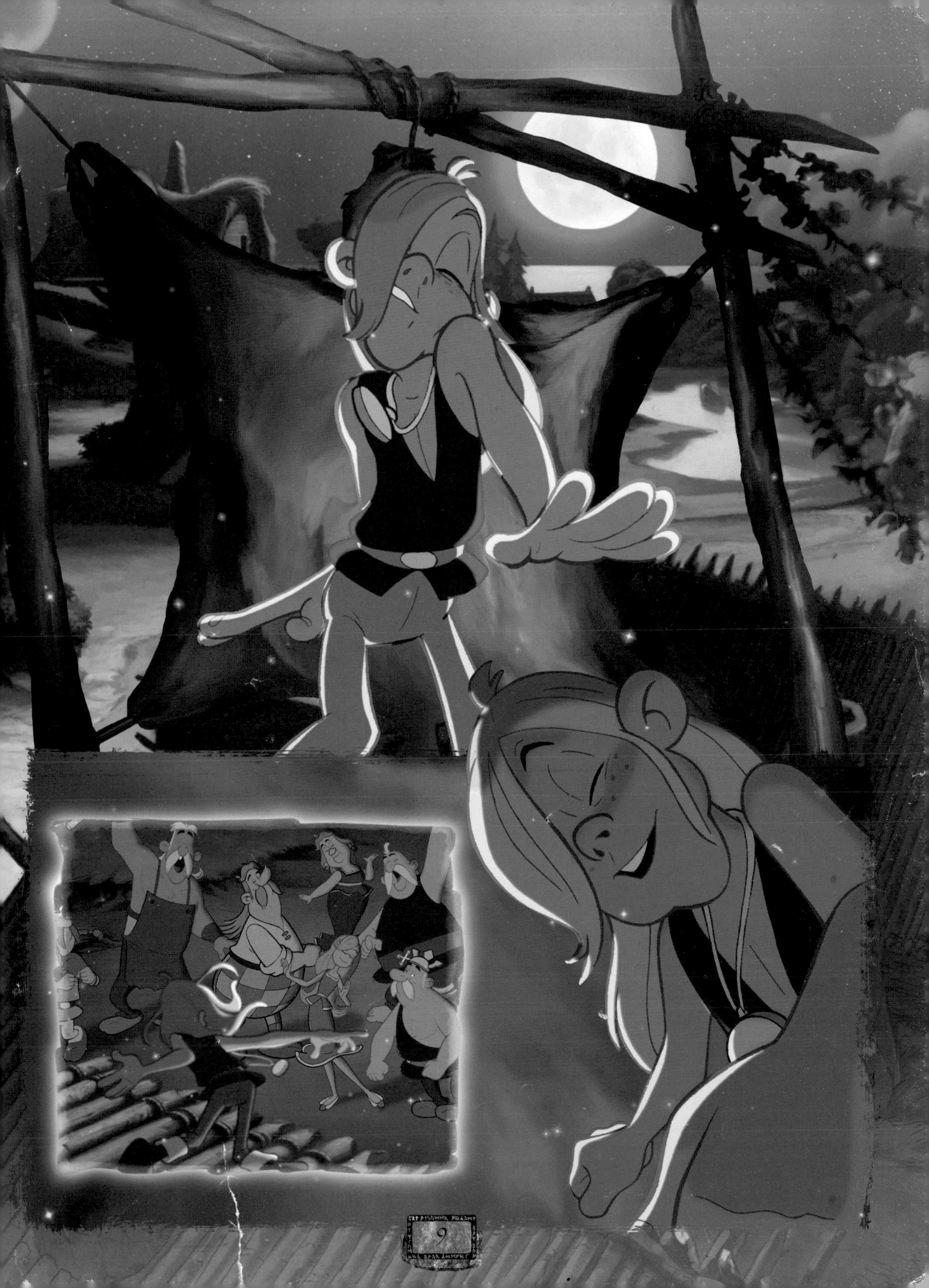

nd far away, at the mouth of a narrow fjord, a longship is putting out to sea. The square sail with its wide vertical stripes unfurls. In single file, the Vikings are carrying their heavy loads aboard the ship. Cryptograf checks that his fool of a son hasn't forgotten anything.

'Club, bludgeon, change of under-armour?'

In his deep, cavernous voice Olaf protests. 'Dad, please! I'm not a kid now, and this isn't my first expedition, you know.'

He's right, it isn't, but there's a lot at stake. Because if Olaf captures the champion of fear he'll get the chief's daughter, he'll get the chief's position, and Cryptograf will get power. All that, however, is rather too complicated for poor Olaf to understand.

Among the crates and chests dumped in the snow near the ship, there is a distinctly sinister item. A cage the right size for a human being is waiting to be taken aboard.

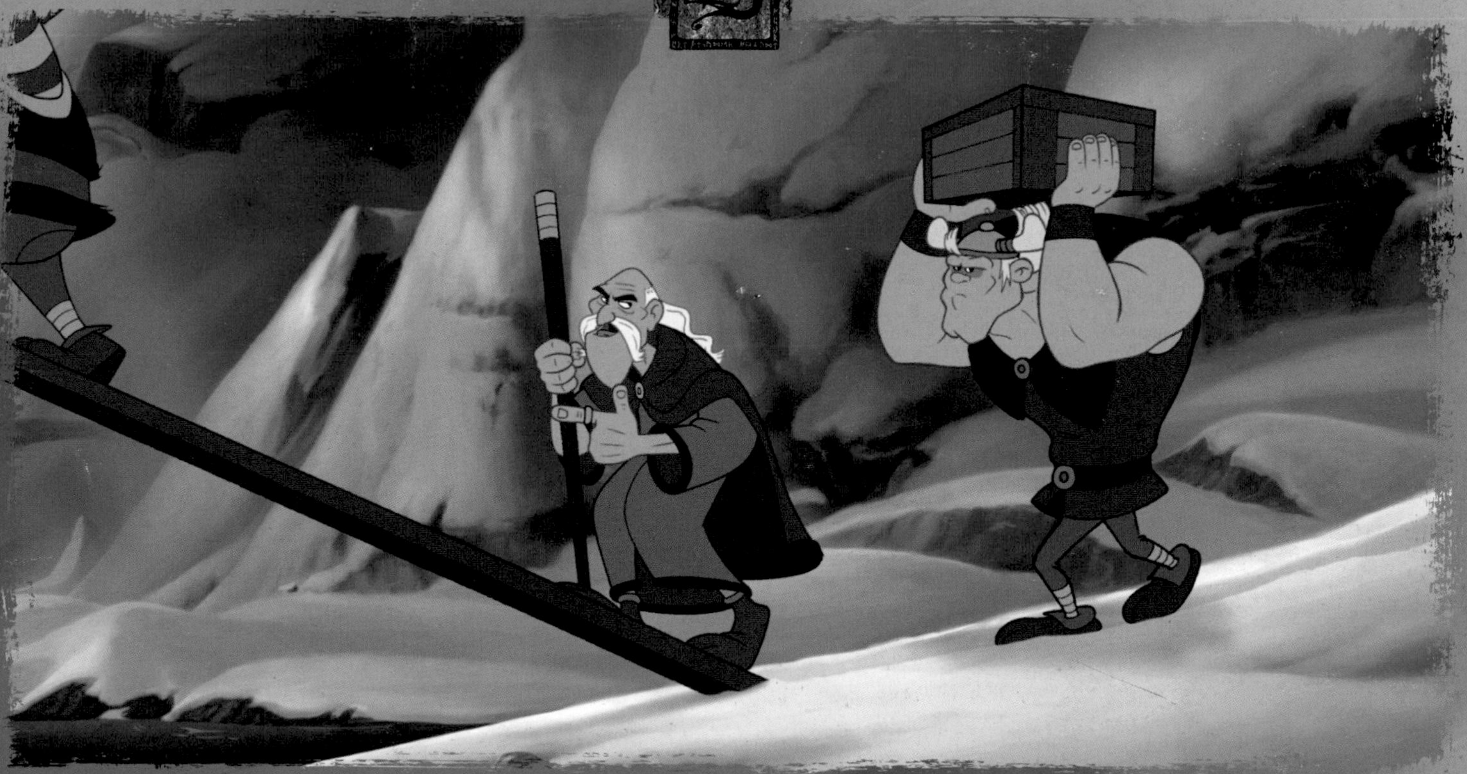

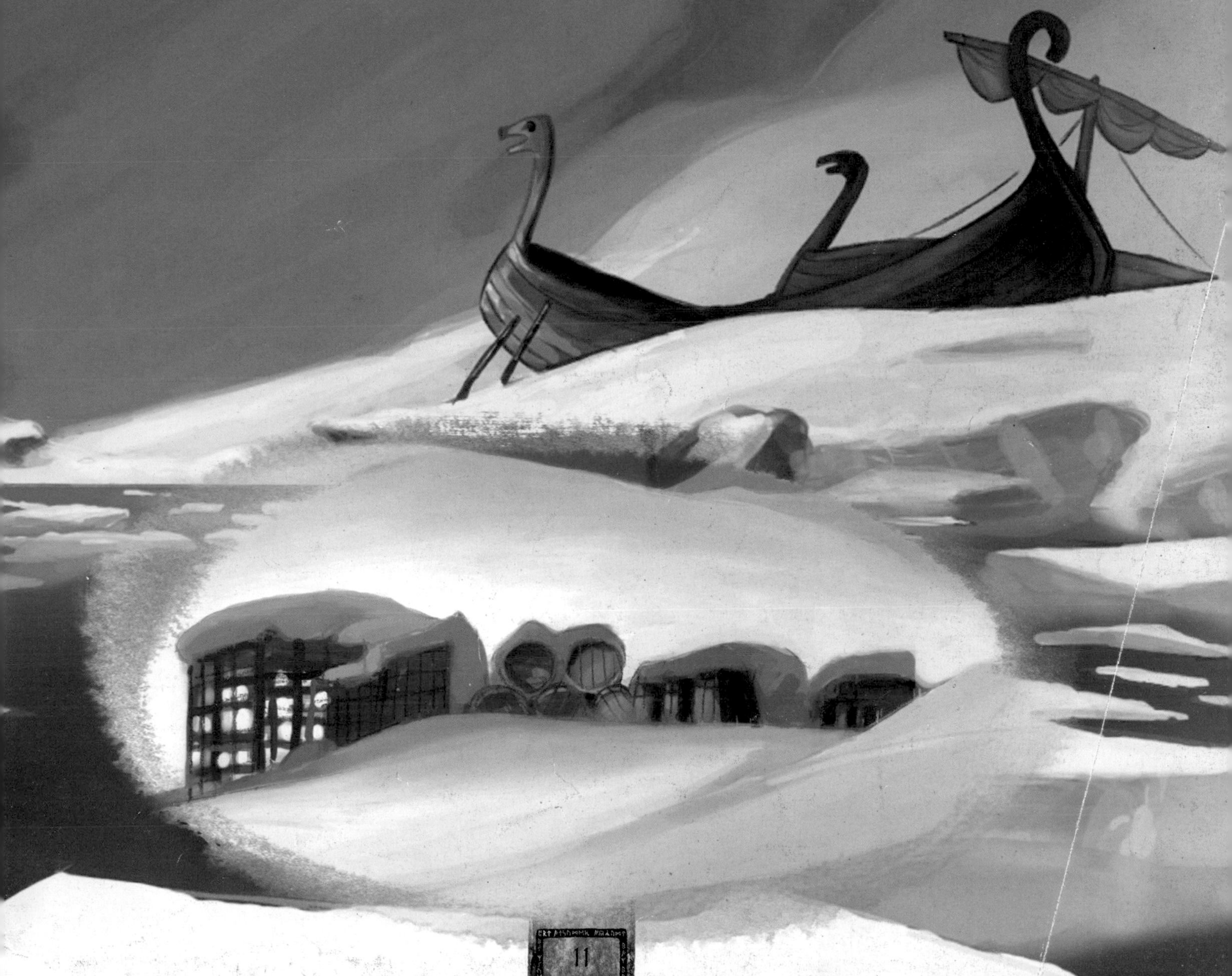

Timandahaf is finishing his preparations. His wife Vikea, a real domestic goddess, gives him a looting list of things to bring home: flat-packed easy self-assembly furniture, candelabras, a set of matching skulls …

The back door is flung open as if by a gust of wind, and in comes a pretty, lively girl with a big trunk on her back, ready for the great adventure. But no way is Timandahaf letting his daughter Abba come too.

'Oh, Dad, pretty please!'

Fluttering eyelashes, a bewitching smile, a loving hand placed on the Viking's manly chest – none of her coaxing works.

'Why on earth would you want to come?'

'Because!'

She's a girl with attitude: after sending her mother's cadaverous crockery flying with a furious kick, she takes a sharp sword to her pillows and her cuddly toys, and soon she's enveloped in a cloud of feathers. When two of them settle under her nose like a moustache, they tickle. That gives her an idea …

And so the oarsmen on the expedition include a slender young man who rows with a firm stroke. A few locks of red hair escape from his helmet, his feathery moustache quivers in the sea breeze, but he keeps going well, no doubt feeling better than the cunning Cryptograf, who is seasick.

Will Cryptograf's cunning plan work? The longship ploughs a furrow through the waves, the clouded sky offers no clues …

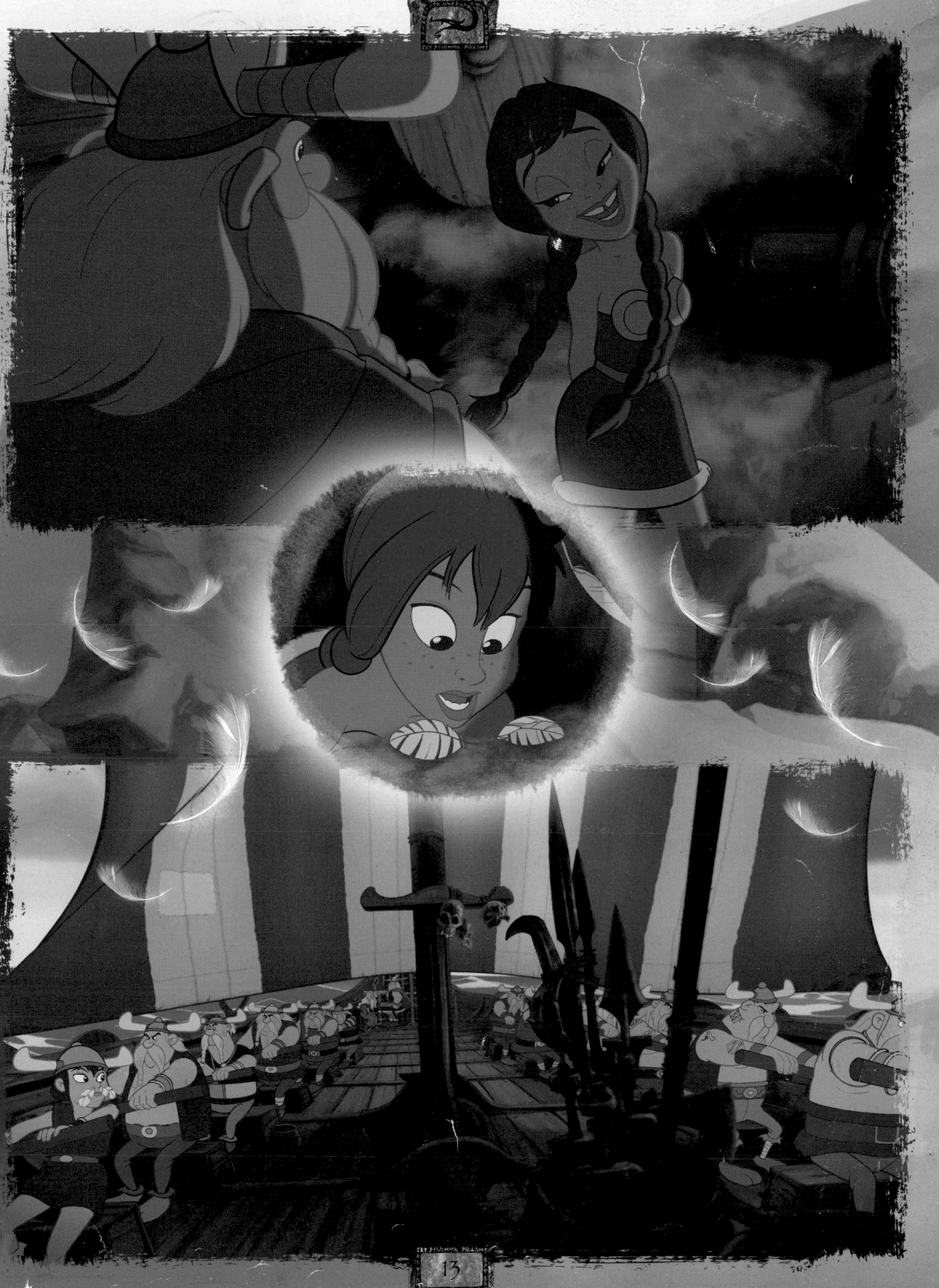

In the peaceful little Gaulish village, the rooster's crow rends the morning air, but nothing wakes Justforkix and SMS up easily. However, the young man's initiation into village life has begun, and everyone knows that the early bird catches the worm. Obelix, a logical thinker, tries the kind of wake-up call that he knows will work: he sends Justforkix flying through the window.

Now the daily routine can begin: there are menhirs to deliver, boars to hunt, pirates to attack. Every new day has its quota of menhirs, boars and pirate fights, and Obelix, as the young man's personal trainer and an excellent teacher, shows him how it's all done. Justforkix takes refuge with his uncle. 'Please don't leave me alone with those lunatics,' he begs.

So Asterix and Obelix are told to find something that Justforkix *does* like to do. They decide to show him round a Roman camp. Justforkix thinks they're going to a party.

Before they leave, they drink a spoonful or so of magic potion from the cauldron.

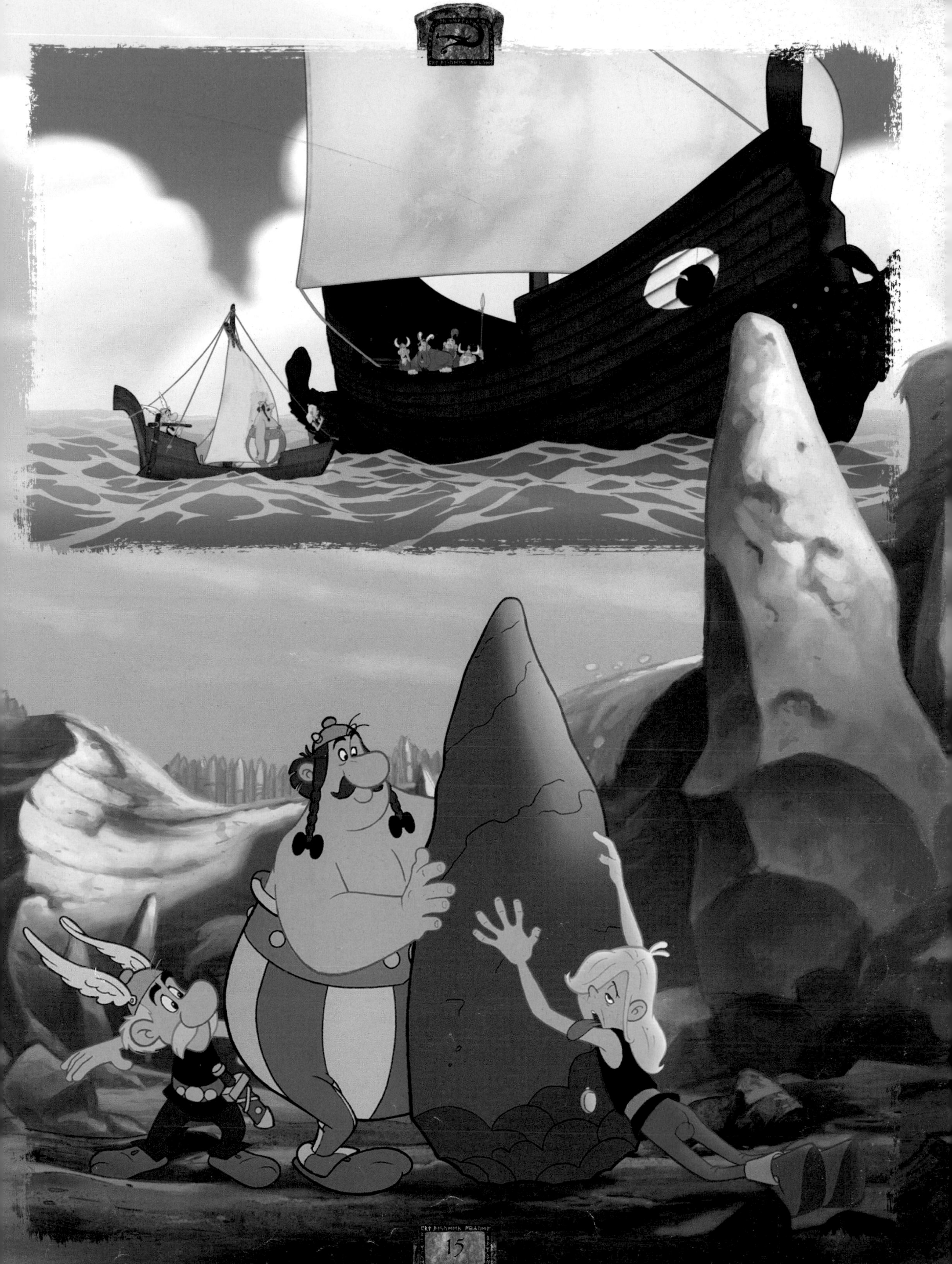

On the longship, Olaf is going down the rows of Viking oarsmen, serving dinner. 'Salmon or salmon?'

'Shalmon!' says the unknown oarsman with the fluffy moustache, indistinctly.

A faint mist is fogging up Olaf's brain. Surely he's never seen this Viking before? At that moment the heavy swell of the sea throws the oarsman overboard. He almost sinks before they fish him out and get him back on deck, dripping with water. It's now that the young man turns out to be a girl … and what a girl!

With a single sword stroke, Timandahaf sends her helmet flying. Her bright red plaits fall to below her waist.

'Abba! I said you couldn't come!'

'I'm sick and tired of staying at home!'

'Well, have you had enough of going to sea now?'

'No way!' And Abba leaps up on the prow, where she makes an eloquent speech. 'Women have a right to learn what fear means too!'

Standing like a superb statue, admired by all the crew and looking like *Liberty Leading the People*,[*] she carries them along with her. 'Onward and upward!' she cries.

Olaf has only just worked it out that this boy is really the chief's daughter when the cry they've all been waiting for rings out.

'Land! Land ahead!'

And they row, row together …

[*] Picture by the famous Gaulish artist Delacrowix

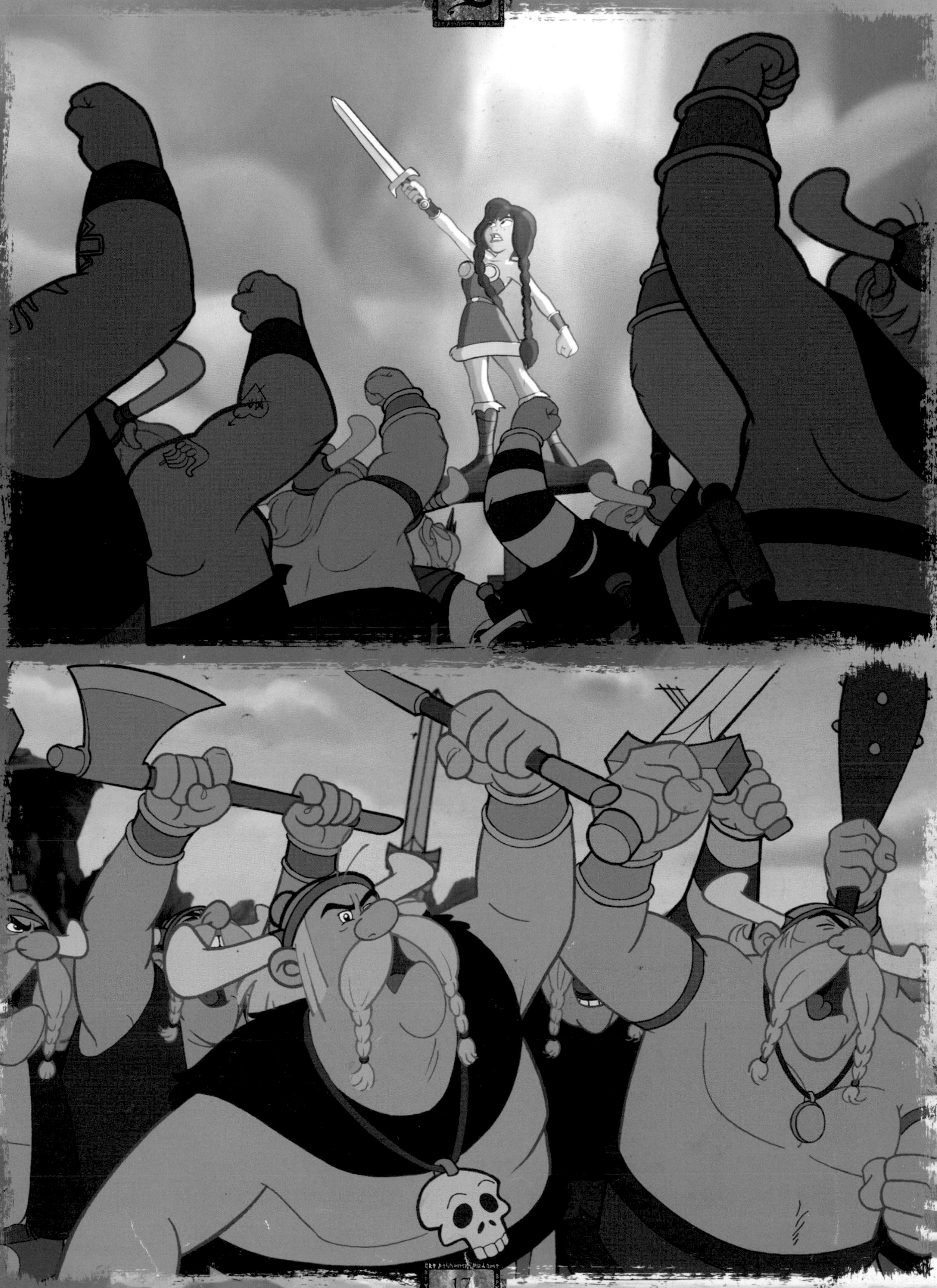

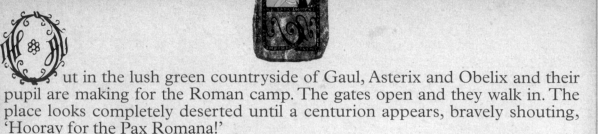

Out in the lush green countryside of Gaul, Asterix and Obelix and their pupil are making for the Roman camp. The gates open and they walk in. The place looks completely deserted until a centurion appears, bravely shouting, 'Hooray for the Pax Romana!'

He's obviously new around here.

'Ssh, Oleaginus, calm down!' mutters the decurion from his hiding place.

Obelix overpowers the eager beaver and hands him to Justforkix.

'Your go now, sonny. I'll count up to three. One …'

But Justforkix is a pacifist …

'Two …'

… and opposed to all forms of physical violence.

'Three! Oh, well done! A promising start!'

Justforkix has had some magic potion, so a tiny little tap knocked the Roman down.

Now for the kind of fun that Asterix and Obelix like! Once the Roman legionaries have formed a crocodile, all the Gauls have to do is bash their orderly ranks until they're flying through the air. It's raining teeth, splintered spears, shields and Romans! But Justforkix doesn't like rain, or this sort of party. He'd rather have a rave. A kindly Roman shows him the exit.

'Second gate on the right.'

Howling with fright, the young man makes for the dark forest. In his headlong flight he sees light in the distance. Over there he'll be sure to find the open sky, the beach, peace and quiet! He collapses on the sand, where his equally scared dove SMS joins him. Getting his breath back, he finally raises his head – and what does he see on the horizon?

'The Vi … the Vi-vi … the Vikings!'

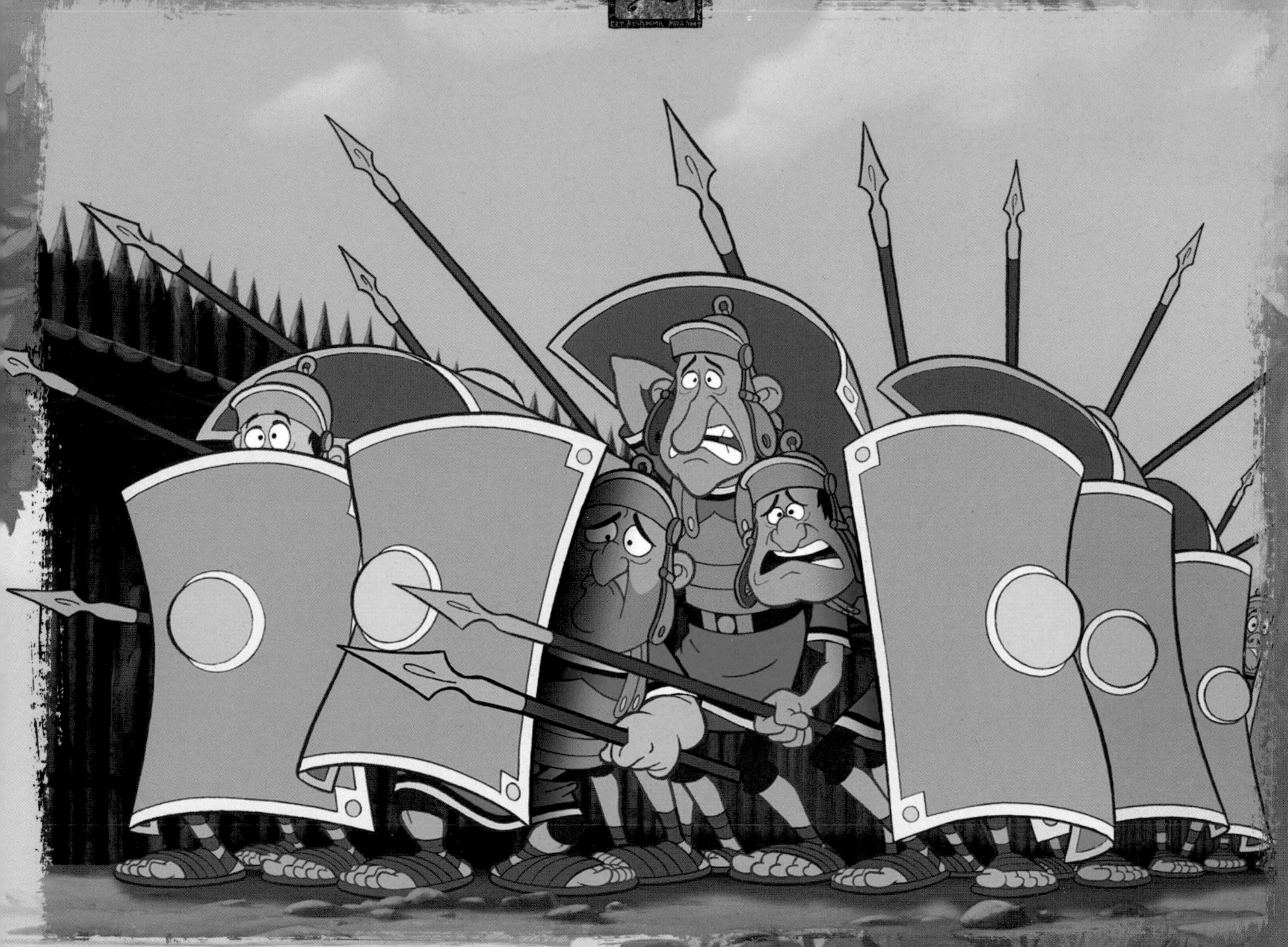

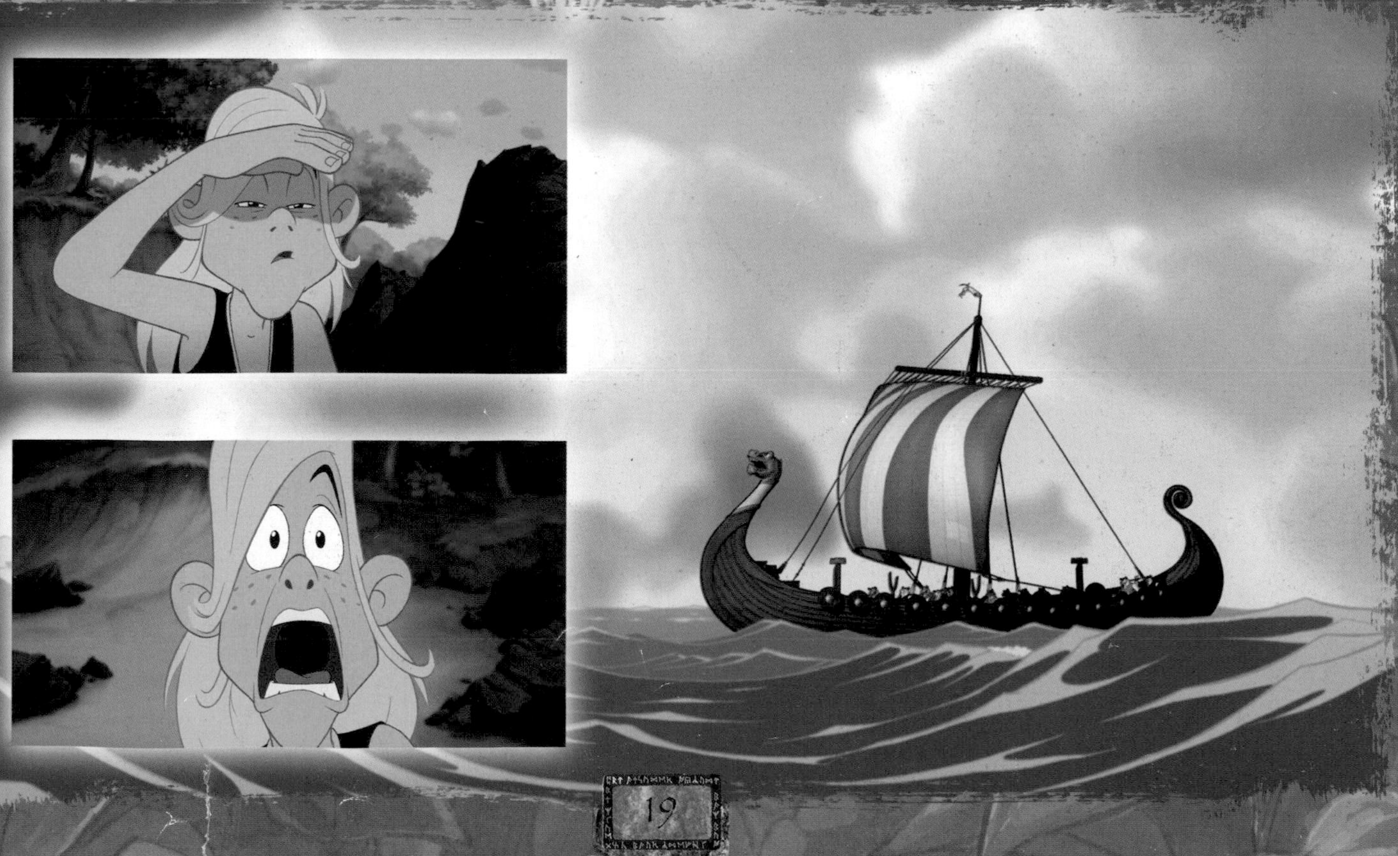

Has he really seen the Vikings? Let's take a closer look ourselves … yes, he's right! The fearless Abba, hanging from the prow of the ship with one hand, looks forward to going ashore. But that's not how her father sees things.

'Don't even think about it, young lady! You're staying here on board!'

'You can't make me!'

'Can't I, though?'

And next moment the girl has been overpowered and shut inside that sinister cage. So much for her bold exploration of enemy territory! So much for her dreams of warlike deeds! Abba is furious. But now Timandahaf can concentrate on addressing his men.

'Right then, no killing and looting for once. This is a study trip. For now, we observe them. The time to slaughter them will come later.'

At these stirring words the Vikings charge off inland, roaring. All of them but Abba, who is left imprisoned on board the longship.

Olaf and Cryptograf have gone a little way from the others, because Cryptograf has something to say to his son. He starts by hitting him on the head with his stick.

'Now, are you sure you understand what we have to do?'

'I'm sorry, Dad,' says Olaf, 'but it's a really complicated plan.'

They are sitting under a couple of trees, facing each other. The soothsayer tries a practical illustration.

'See this stone? That's you. And see that one? It's the champion of fear. If you capture him you'll get to marry the chief's daughter. This is the chief's daughter.'

'Looks like another rock to me.'

'No, it's a girl now! And if you marry her you get to be chief after Chief Timandahaf. Got the idea, son?'

'Er … yes. I'm solid rock.'

Well, perhaps Olaf has grasped the basics.

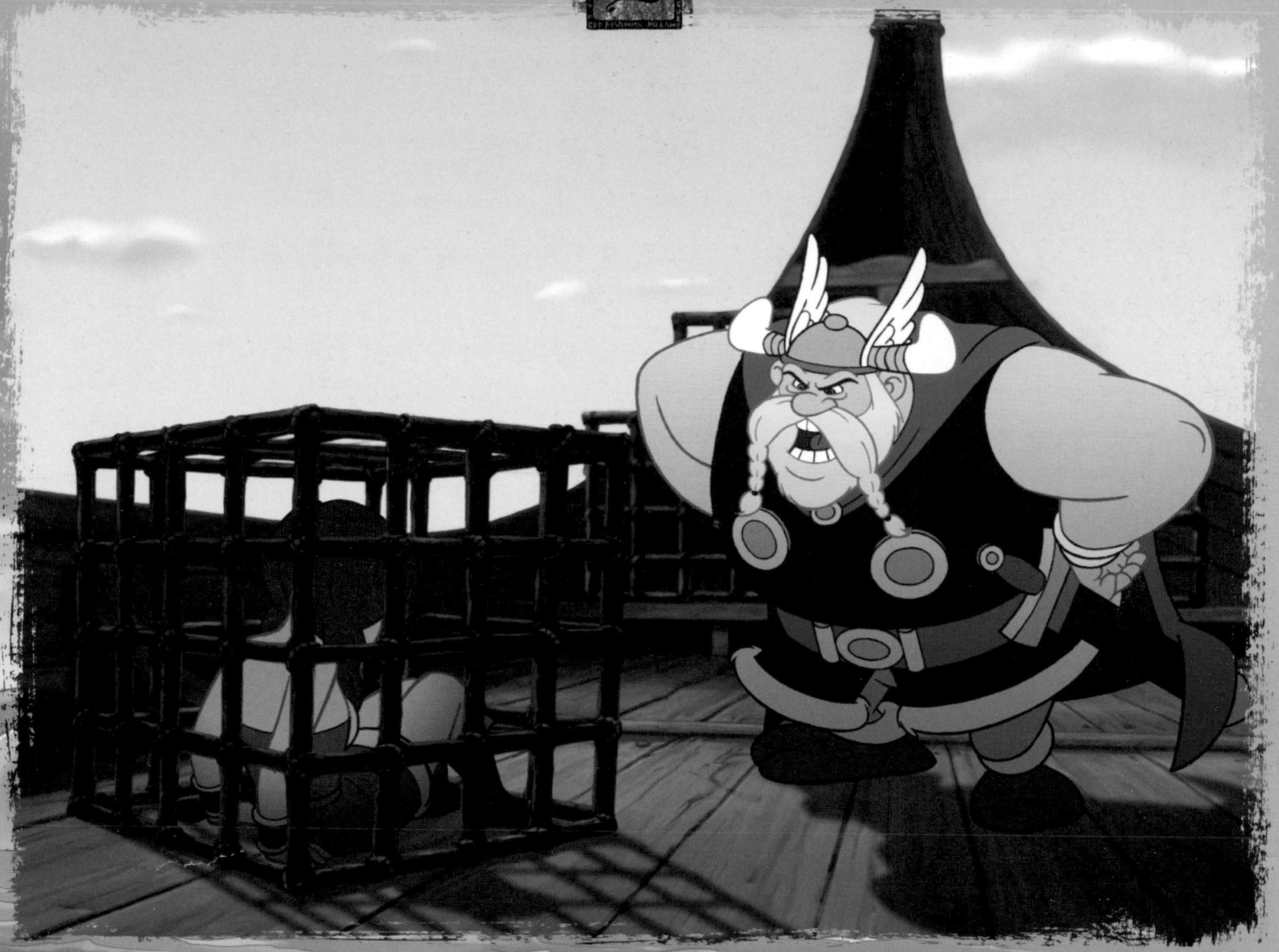

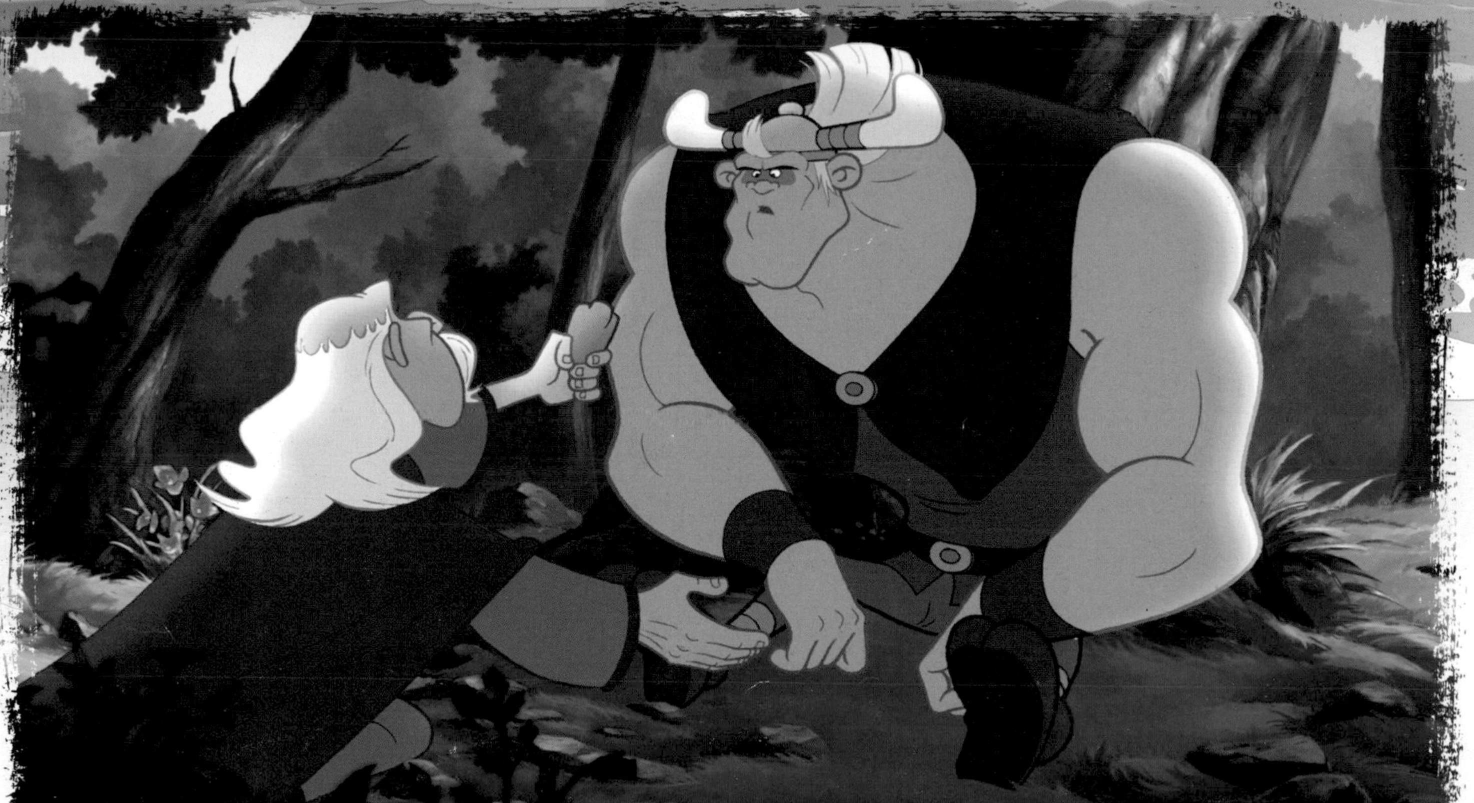

Back in the Roman camp, Obelix and Asterix are finishing their demolition job when Justforkix arrives at a run. 'The Vikings are coming!'

But the two Gauls just calmly finish off what they are doing.

'Vikings, did you say? Well, bloodthirsty brutes they may be, but they'll just have to wait their turn like everyone else!'

The young man starts off back to the forest in despair. There are glints of light in the darkness, sounds, a pair of eyes … and the eyes belong to Olaf, who is spying out the land. Suddenly feeling worried about Justforkix, Asterix and Obelix catch up with him.

'Don't be frightened. We're here to help you. We're Gauls, remember? We don't know the meaning of fear!'

'Speak for yourselves,' says Justforkix. 'I do. I'm frightened of everything … I'm a real champion of fear!'

Olaf's eyebrows come together, his mouth drops open. He's actually found the champion of fear! Here he is, just a couple of paces away! But what are those two Gauls doing? Reassuring him? That's sabotage!

Olaf hurries off to tell Chief Timandahaf about his discovery. The chief isn't pleased.

'You think we came here just to eat Gaulish pancakes and take notes? Why didn't you grab him? Go and get that champion before the Gauls turn him brave!'

'Yes, Chief,' says Olaf.

While the Gaulish village comes to life, Justforkix is harnessing the horses to his chariot. Obelix goes over to him, putting on his shoes and sketching a few dance steps. But the young man can't be persuaded to stay. Regretfully, Obelix goes to find him a goodbye present.

'This is for you. One training session a day and you'll soon be able to lift it!' he says, giving Justforkix his very best menhir.

'Lift that?' says the young man, discouraged. 'It's impossible!'

'How can you say something's impossible if you've never tried it?'

(Please don't forget that remark … it's going to be important in this story.)

Now Asterix arrives. He isn't pleased, and says Justforkix must stay. And while the two friends are arguing Justforkix drives away, taking the menhir.

Once again he races at high speed through the dark forest. He is standing up to drive his chariot when a wheel suddenly comes off. The chariot skids and its frame collapses.

'My lovely new sports chariot! That crummy menhir!'

And there's no one around to help. No one? A slight breeze, small sounds, maybe small squirrels? A little echo? A shadow?

'Eeek! A Viking! A fist! A …'

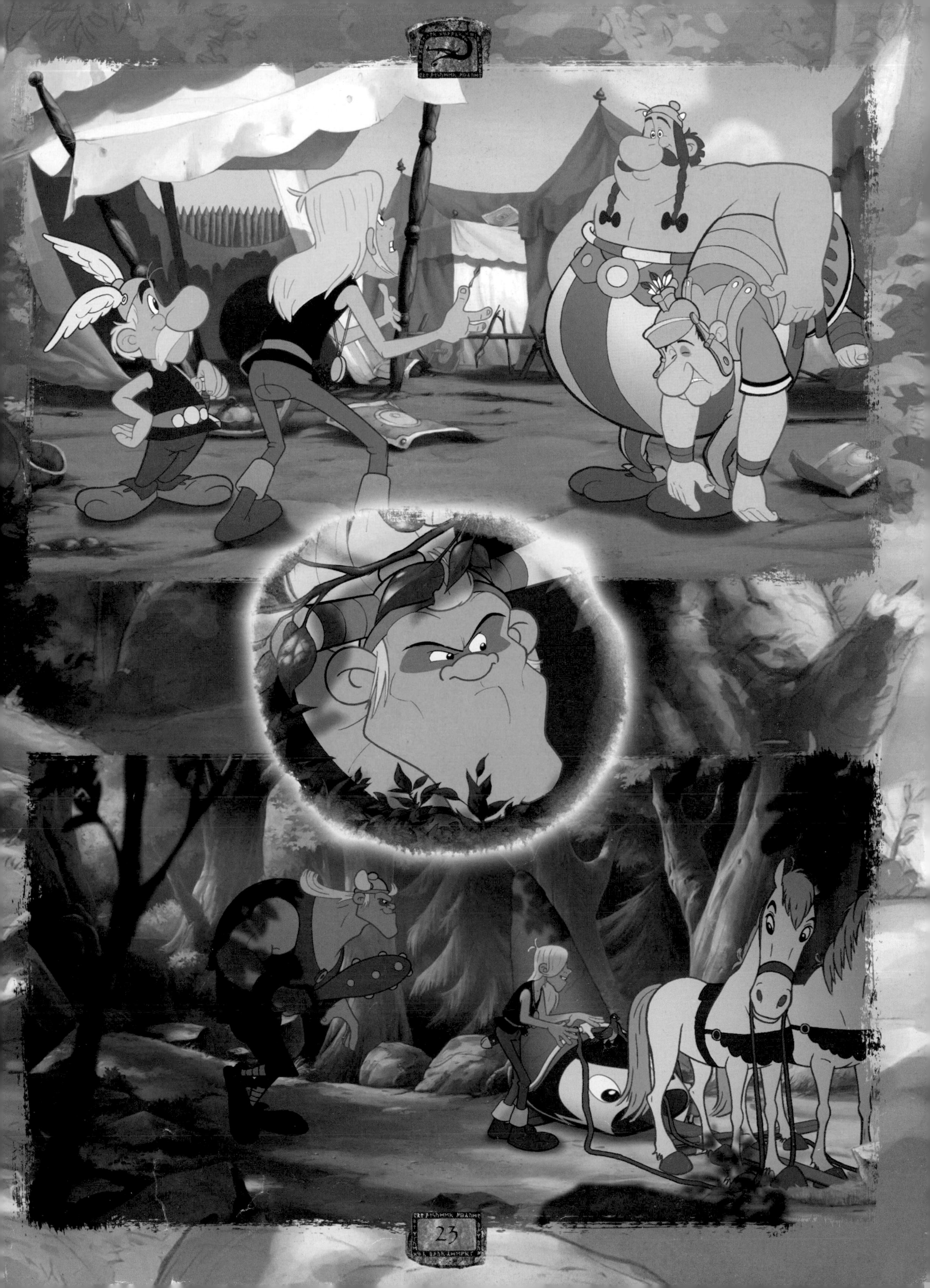

Sitting on the bench outside their hut, Asterix and Obelix are brooding gloomily. Anyone can see that Obelix is sad about the sudden way Justforkix left. He isn't even hungry. The friends feel remorseful, regretting what might have been. Asterix is trying to cheer his friend up when SMS arrives in a flurry of dove wings.

'What's going on?'

Dogmatix deciphers the message she has brought and passes the news on. 'Justforkix has had an accident.'

They hurry through the forest, but there's no one there! They race to the seashore! Past the green trees, they see a panorama of sea and sky, perfectly calm.

But there's a terrible sight on the beach at their feet: a wrecked chariot, and the remains of Justforkix's sword. There's no doubt about it – the Vikings have kidnapped him. They must go back to the village at once to warn Chief Vitalstatistix.

And guess who's visiting the village? Justforkix's father, come to see how his son is doing! Asterix and Obelix, as the boy's personal trainers, can't possibly tell Doublehelix the whole truth. They pretend he's gone on a field trip as part of his training, and his father, reassured, roars with laughter and says he'll be back at the next full moon.

Now they must go after the Vikings as fast as possible, rescue the young man and bring him back before his father returns at the time of the full moon. Asterix and Obelix go aboard a ship to embark on their new mission: saving the life of the chief's nephew and the honour of the village.

All they have to do now is find the sea route leading to the icy Arctic lands. Their frail craft, heavily laden with stocks of wild boar, must follow the North Star.

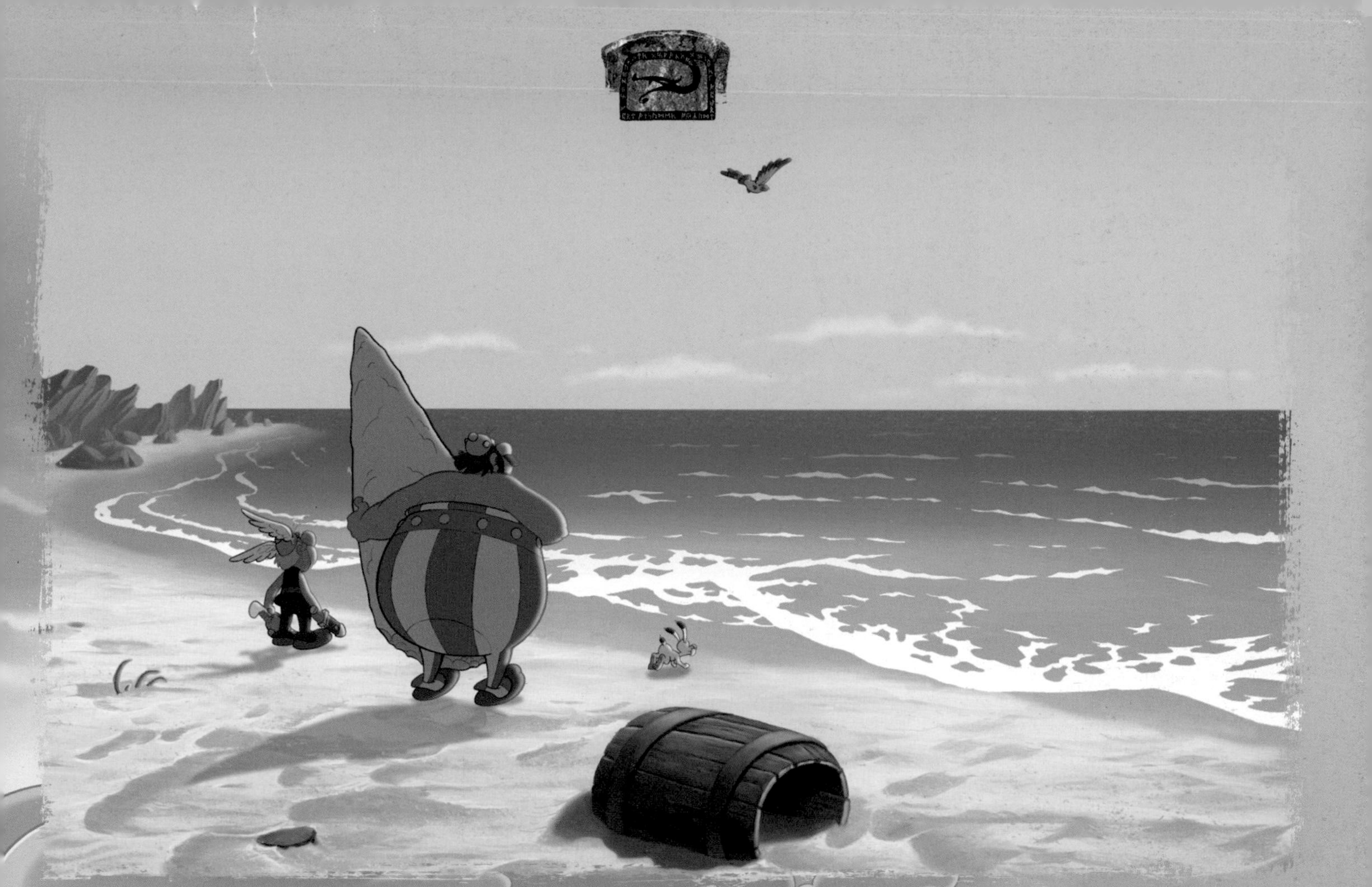

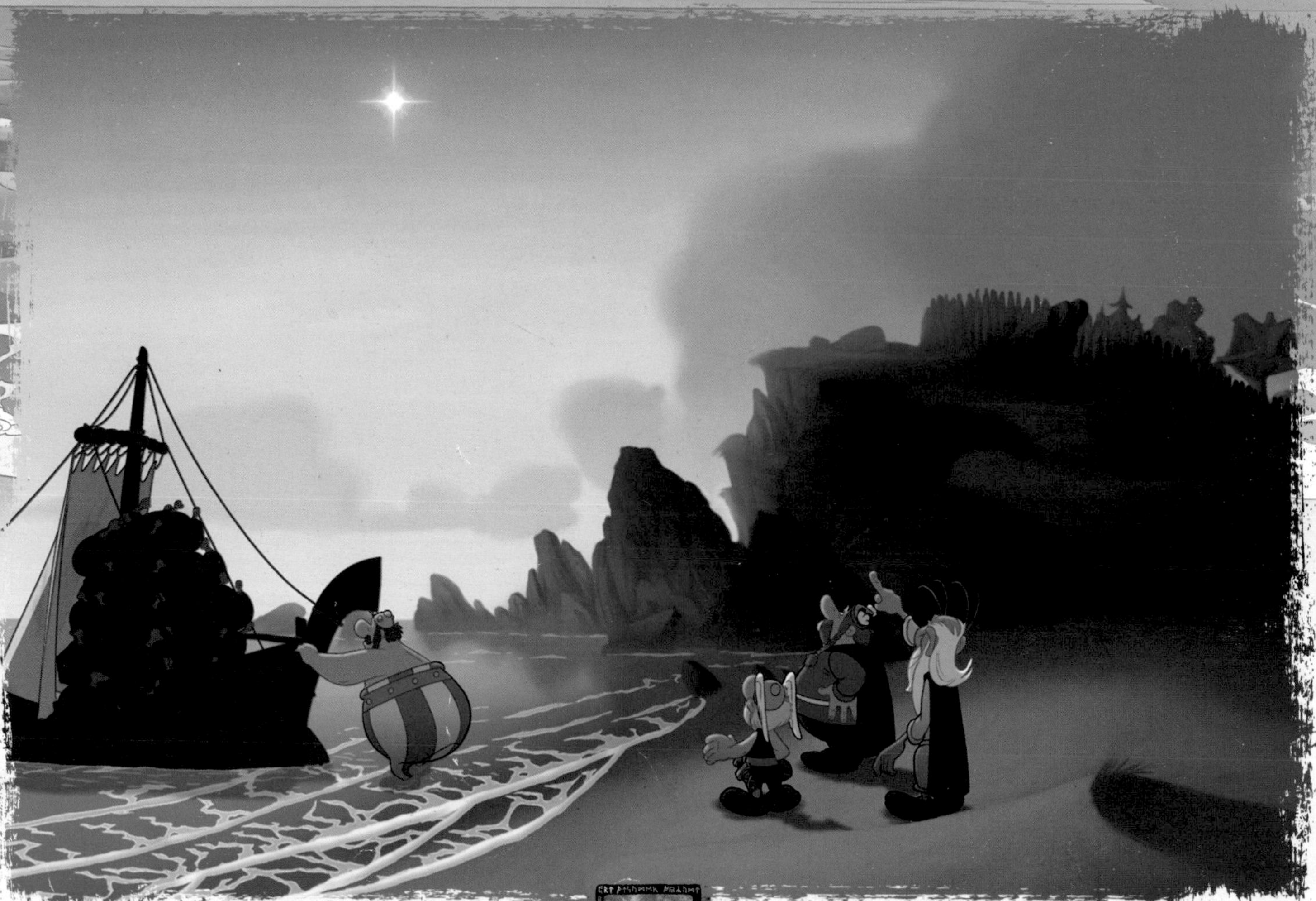

Justforkix, who has fainted, is lying on the deck of the longship. A bucket of icy water in the face brings him round, and he finds himself surrounded by horned helmets, terrifying jaws, gigantic bodies and heaps and heaps of skulls.

'Mercy!' he begs.

'Mercy? What's that?' ask the Viking study group.

'Must be one of their newfangled inventions!'

Their mission isn't to take an interest in mercy, so they tie their prisoner up tightly – because, don't forget, it's his ability to fly that makes him so valuable to them.

Some way off, the Gaulish ship has gone off course in fog, a real pea-souper. The Gauls have lost sight of the North Star. As Asterix peers through the fog, Obelix complains that he's starving, and wishes they hadn't exhausted their provisions so soon. He ate all the boars without stopping to work out how long they might be at sea.

But homing in on the Viking longship, SMS swoops through the fog and settles on deck beside her friend. Justforkix smiles. Suddenly a red bombshell explodes next to him.

'Hey, I like your bird!'

'Who are you?'

'I'm Abba.' Then she sees that the precious champion is trembling! Abba takes off her cloak and puts it gently over him, revealing herself in full combat gear.

'It's not the cold,' the young man protests feebly, 'it's fear. I'm so scared.'

'Oh, aren't you lucky! Will you teach me the meaning of fear too? I'd love to fly.'

'Er … well, if you'll help me, I'll try my best.'

Delighted, Abba takes SMS by the feet, and the two of them twirl about in front of the unfortunate champion. He's bowled over. And then – guess what? Fathers always choose just the wrong moment to break the spell.

'What do you think you're doing, Abba? How many times have I told you not to talk to strangers?'

Abba turns away with dignity. Justforkix watches her go, while SMS collapses on deck.

What will become of them?

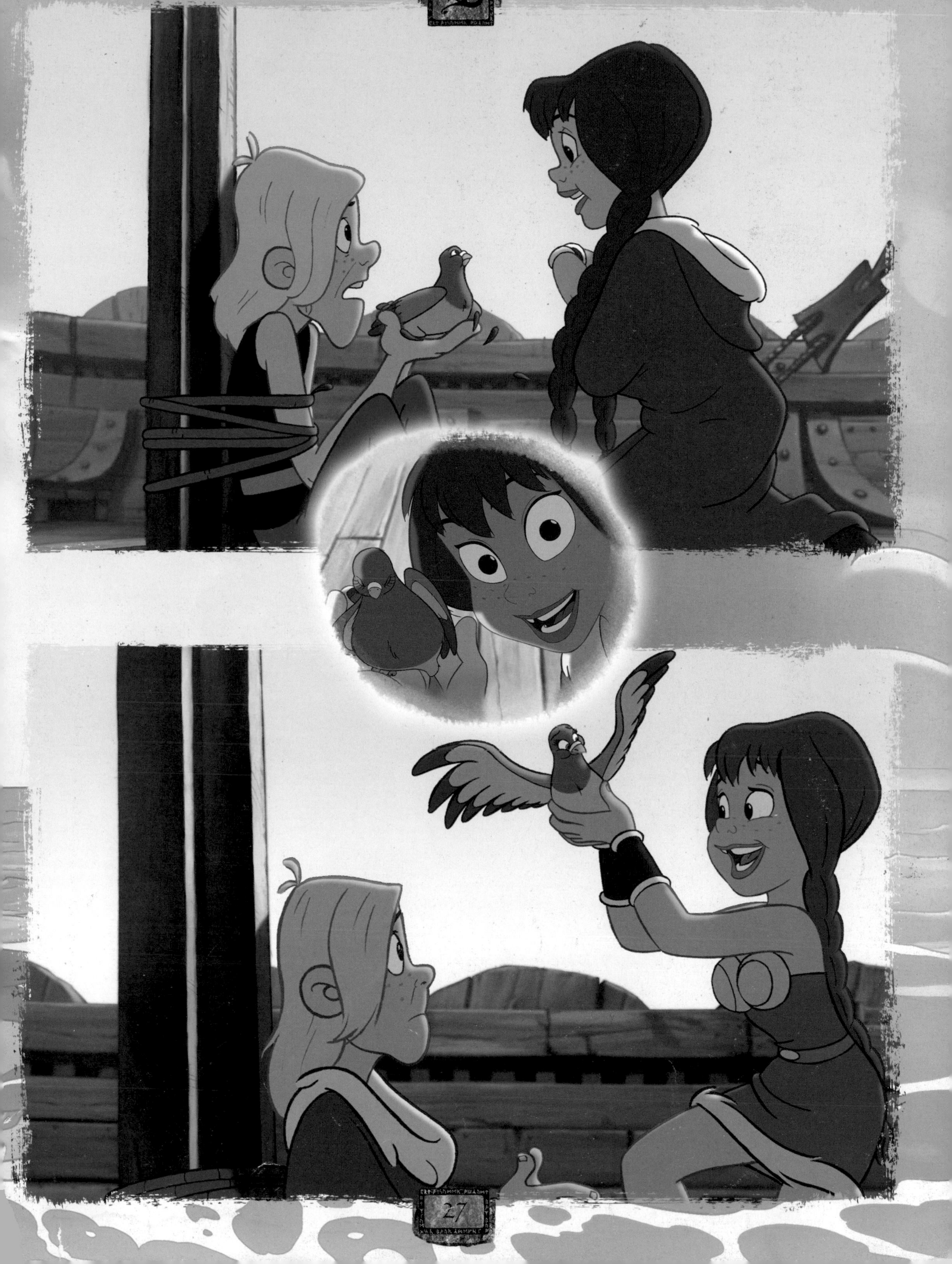

$\mathcal{I}$n the fog, things are getting even worse. Really worried now, Obelix wonders out loud where the North Star has gone.

'By Toutatis!' says Asterix. 'You've just given me a good idea! Throw me up as high as you can, Obelix!'

Asterix flies through the thick cloud layer like an arrow, before dropping back.

'Do it again!' he says. And what should he see this time, high in the sky, but the North Star.

'We go thataway!'

And the ship moves on, this time in the right direction.

$\mathbf{T}$he Vikings are home again. With Abba beside him, Justforkix gets to know the amazing blue and white world of the Arctic. But one thing bothers him: the promise he made to teach her how to fly. Justforkix has come a long way since he was last in Lutetia. He knows now that every nation has its own laws and customs. And he wonders what Vikings do to liars.

'See that skeleton?' asks Abba. 'Over there, frozen into that ice floe. That's the last man who lied to me. Dad punished him as he deserved!'

Poor Justforkix! What can he do but keep up the lies and empty promises?

'How about Tuesday at three in the afternoon for your first flying lesson?'

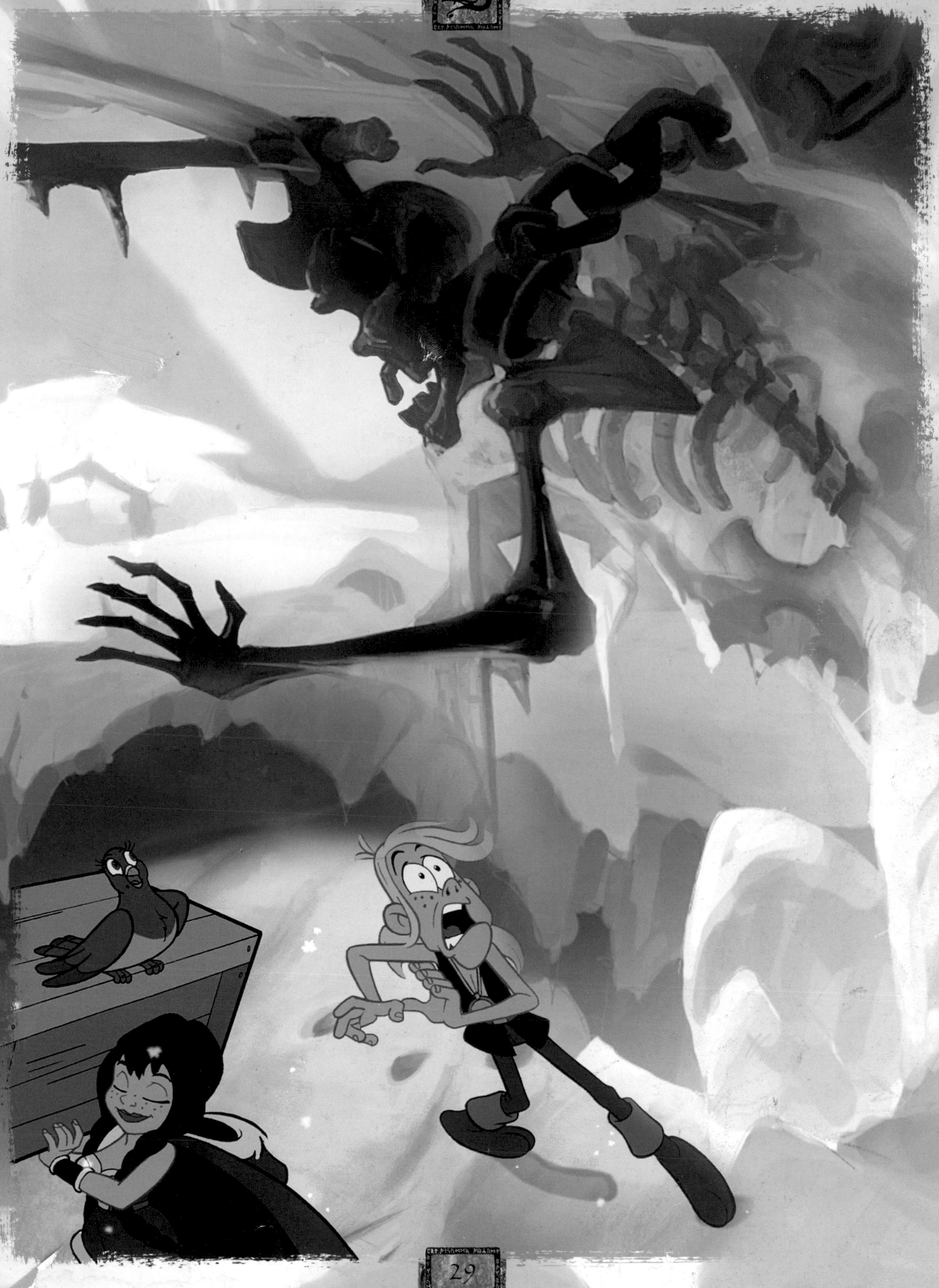

'Let's raise our skulls to toast the champion of fear!' says Timandahaf. The drink is rather strong at first, but his hosts seem so pleased to have him there that Justforkix feels better.

Meanwhile a small ship reaches land at the entrance to the fjord. Asterix and Obelix march through the snow to the door of a large building where the Vikings are queuing up, men with names like Telegraf, Stenograf, Caraf, Nescaf. Obelix thinks those names ending in 'af' are funny, and roars with laughter. There's obviously a big party going on inside the banqueting hall ahead of them. The doorman doesn't want to let them in, but a mighty punch from Asteraf, as he decides to call himself, settles the minor matter of an invitation card. Taking his cue from his friend, Obelaf hands out the strong stuff to anyone who wants a punch. Then the prospect of a delicious dish of creamed walrus calms everyone down.

But not for long …

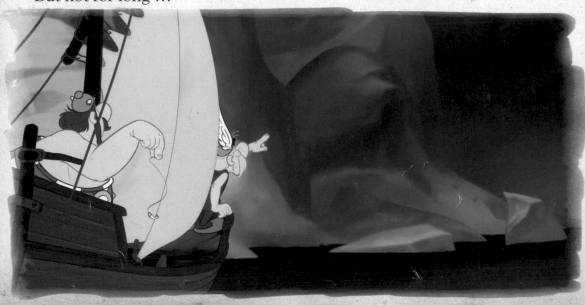

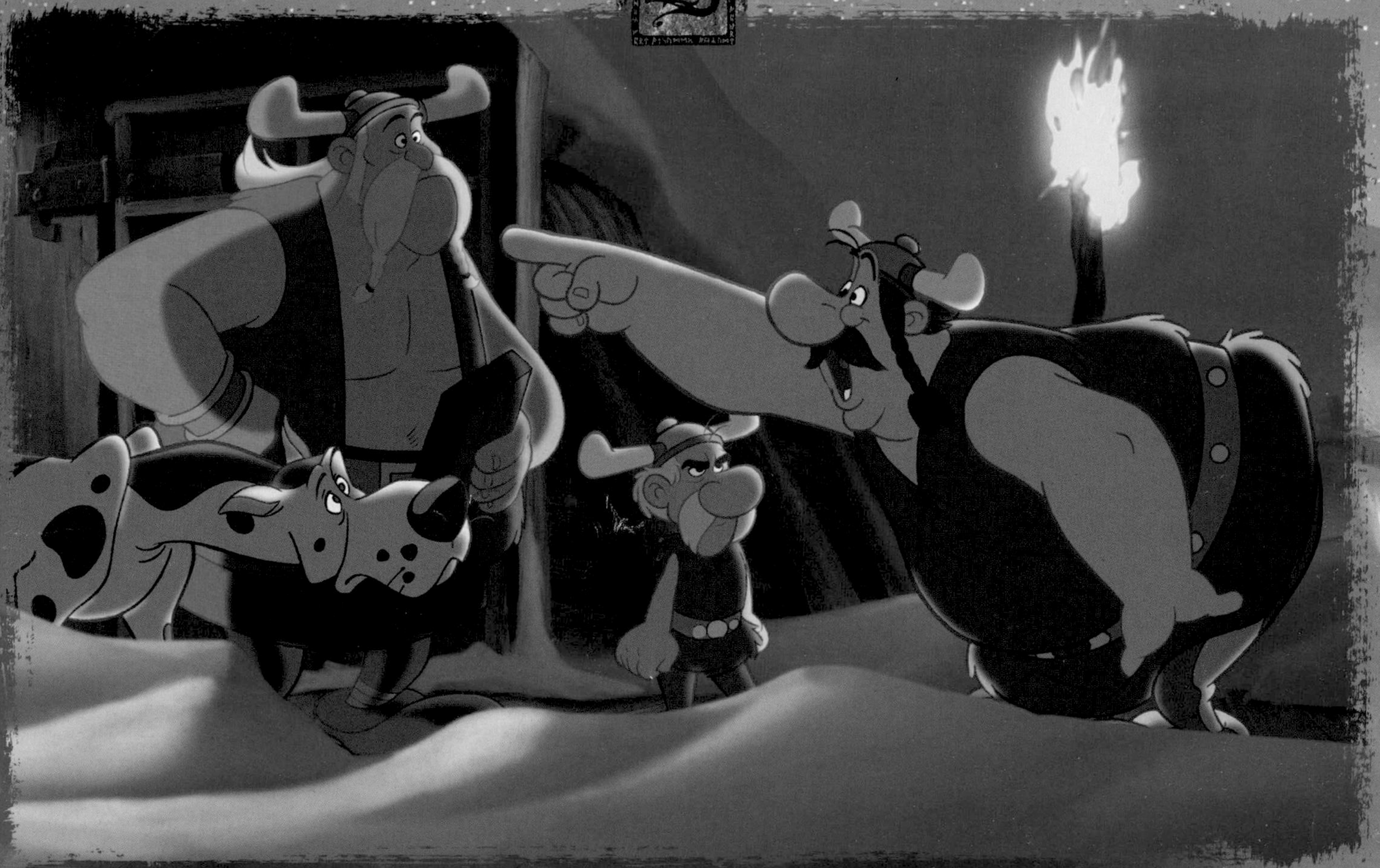

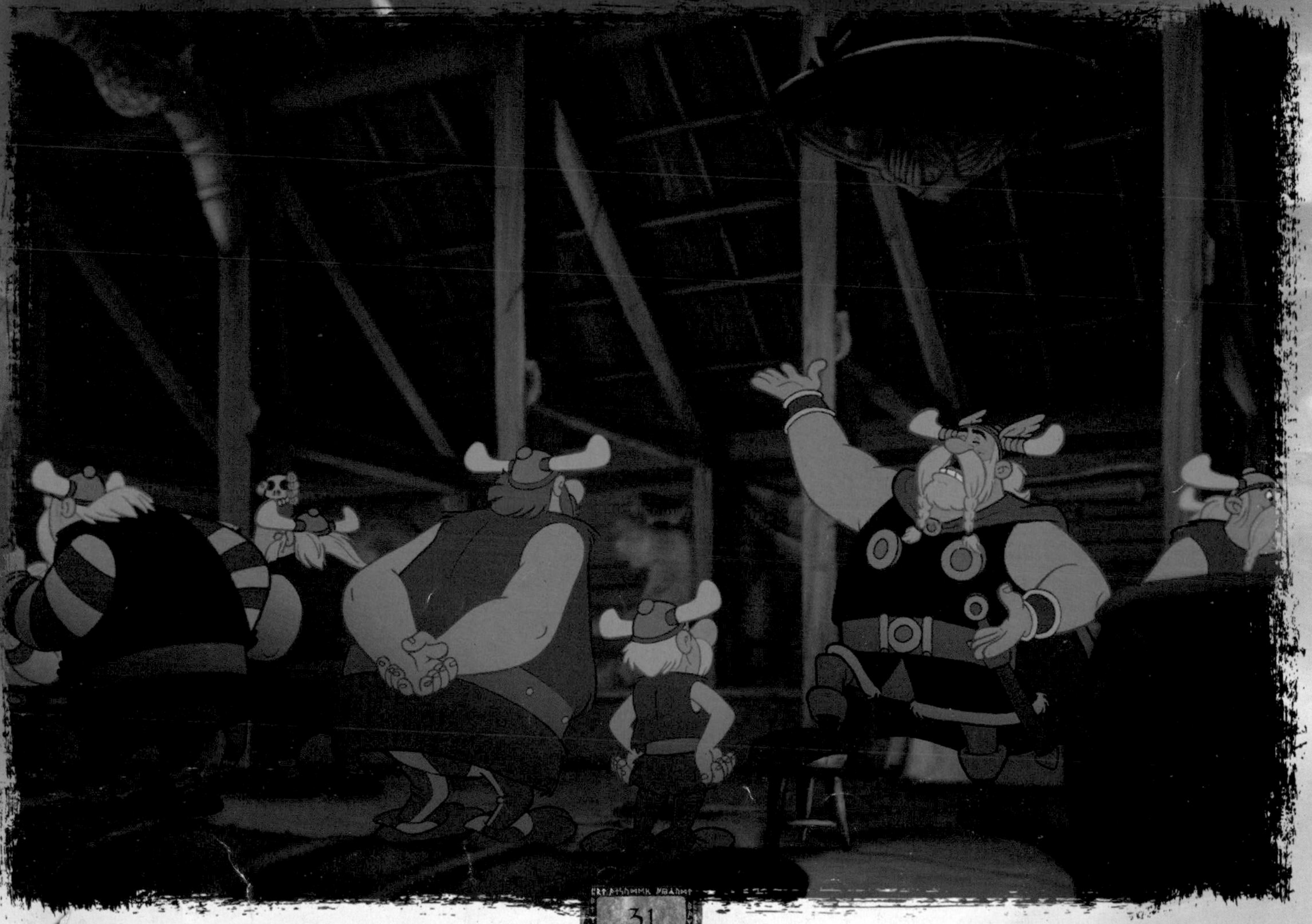

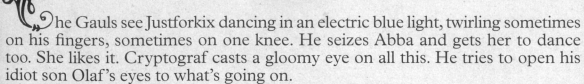

The Gauls see Justforkix dancing in an electric blue light, twirling sometimes on his fingers, sometimes on one knee. He seizes Abba and gets her to dance too. She likes it. Cryptograf casts a gloomy eye on all this. He tries to open his idiot son Olaf's eyes to what's going on.

'Can't you see he's going to steal your fiancée, you total fool?'

Olaf doesn't see it.

This is Justforkix's moment of glory. His audience hoist him on their shoulders in triumph. And as usual, just when young people are having fun … guess what? Along comes Dad or the teacher to spoil everything!

In this case it's Obelix who feels that, as Justforkix's personal trainer, he should come to the rescue. He grabs the boy, picks him up like a feather, and carries him off.

'Hey, I only just got here!' protests Justforkix.

After all his hardships he was beginning to dance and enjoy himself, and now the Gauls want to stop him, saying it's for his father. The father who'd like to be rid of him!

'Because if he didn't,' he tells them, 'he'd never have sent me to visit you lot! You great oafs! You country bumpkins!'

That cruel remark strikes home. Obelix opens his mouth and then closes it again. Wasn't there some ancient Germanic philosopher who said, 'Whereof one cannot speak, thereof one must be silent'? That's just how Obelix feels. Deeply wounded, he turns on his heel and marches away.

Seeing his Gaulish friends go, Justforkix is sorry for what he said and wants to apologise. He runs after them. Abba is baffled, but she follows him.

'Go on, give me a smile!' she begs. 'Pretty please!'

Yes, what do such squabbles mean when Abba is here? Justforkix's feet are freezing in the snow, but his heart is burning … and that first kiss sweeps him away through space and time!

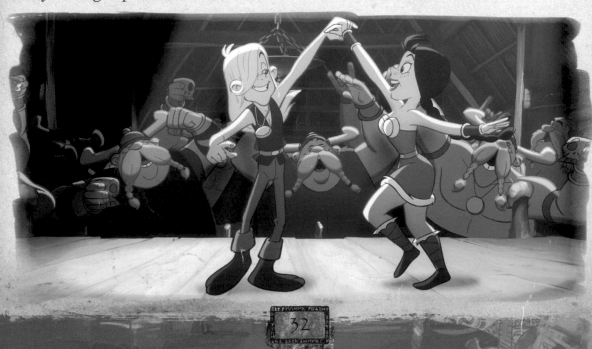

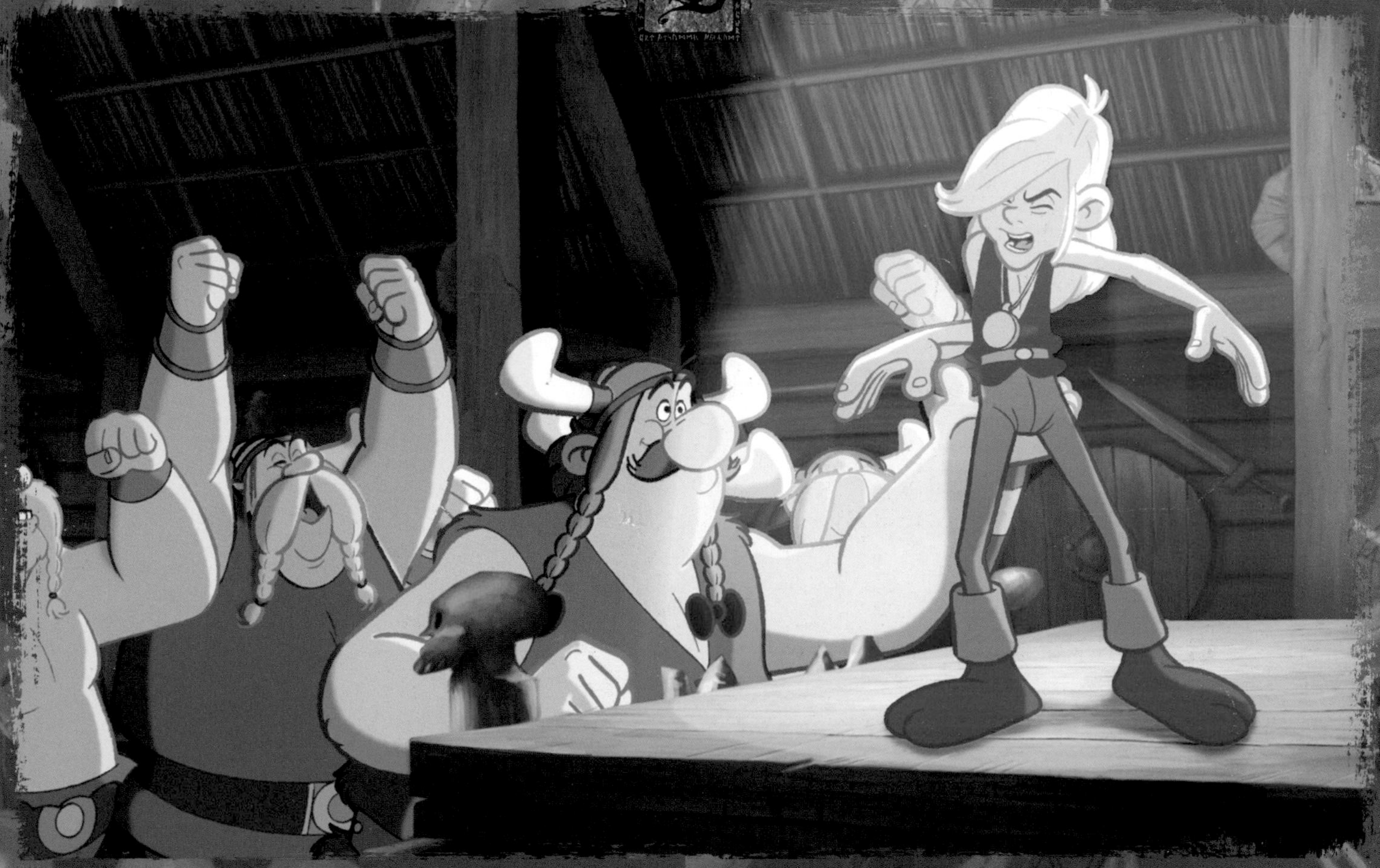

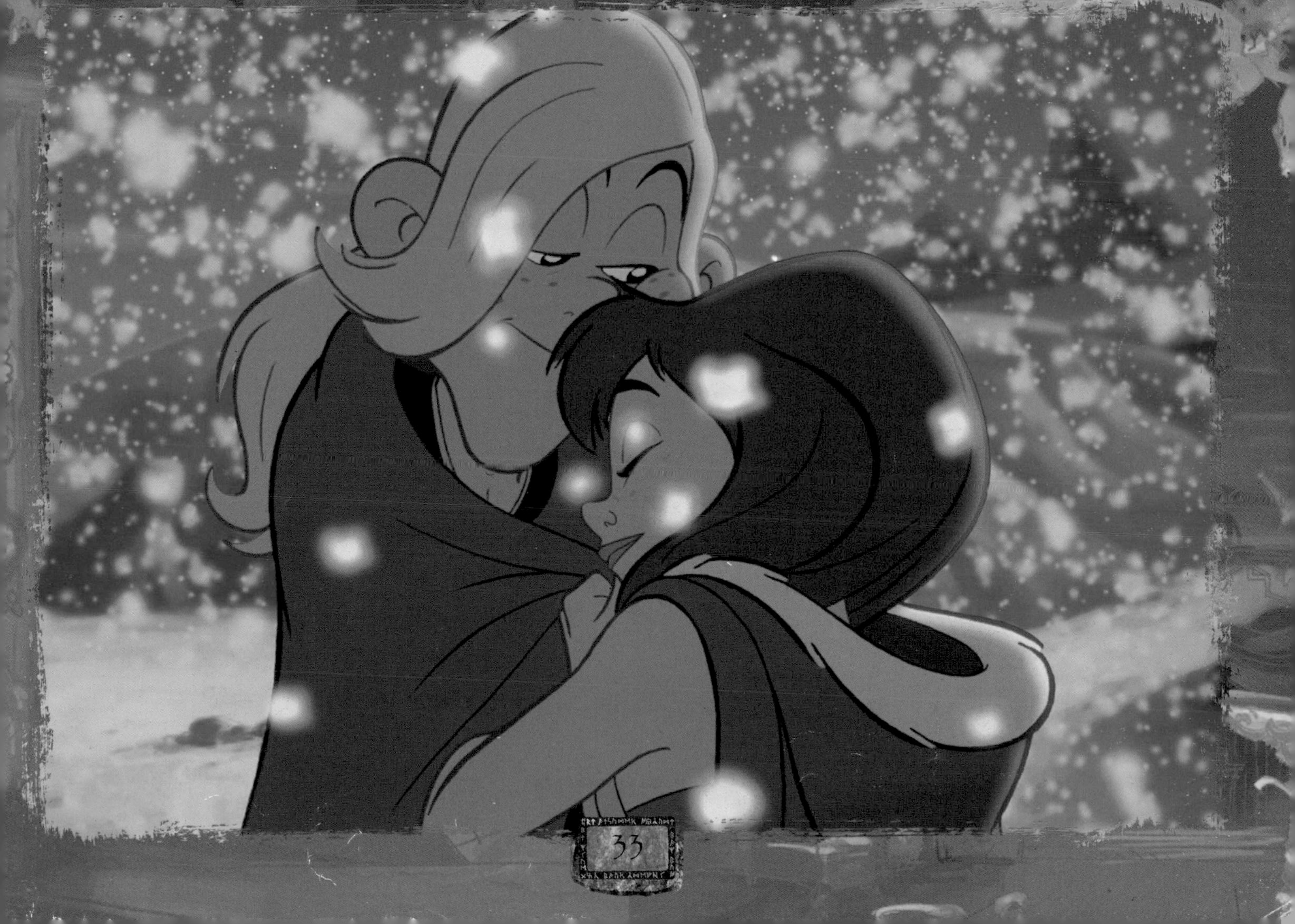

ryptograf decides it's time he put his plan into practice.

'And now let's drink a toast to the heroic Olaf, the man who captured the champion of fear!' he announces. 'You haven't forgotten your promise, I hope, Chief Timandahaf?'

'A chief always keeps his word, by Thor! What would that lad of yours like?'

'My son has the honour of asking for your daughter's hand in marriage!'

At this crucial moment Abba comes up. 'What's all this about marriage?' she enquires.

'None of your business, young lady!' And Timandahaf reminds her that in Viking tradition, a man just drags his intended bride away to her new home by the hair.

But Abba rebels. 'I'm not going to marry that herring brain!'

'Oh yes, you are going to marry that herring brain!'

At least father and daughter agree on the subject of herrings.

Out loud, Abba's mother Vikea remembers her own wedding day, her grazed knees, bruises all over her … the happiest day of her life!

But now Justforkix speaks up. 'Er … may I say something?'

The answer is no. Timandahaf is the chief around here. At a sign from him, guards grab the young couple and tear them apart.

'Tomorrow would be a good day for the wedding, don't you think?' suggests Cryptograf.

'Yes, fine,' agrees the chief. 'But first the champion must show us how to fly!'

Oh dear … Cryptograf hadn't foreseen that little difficulty.

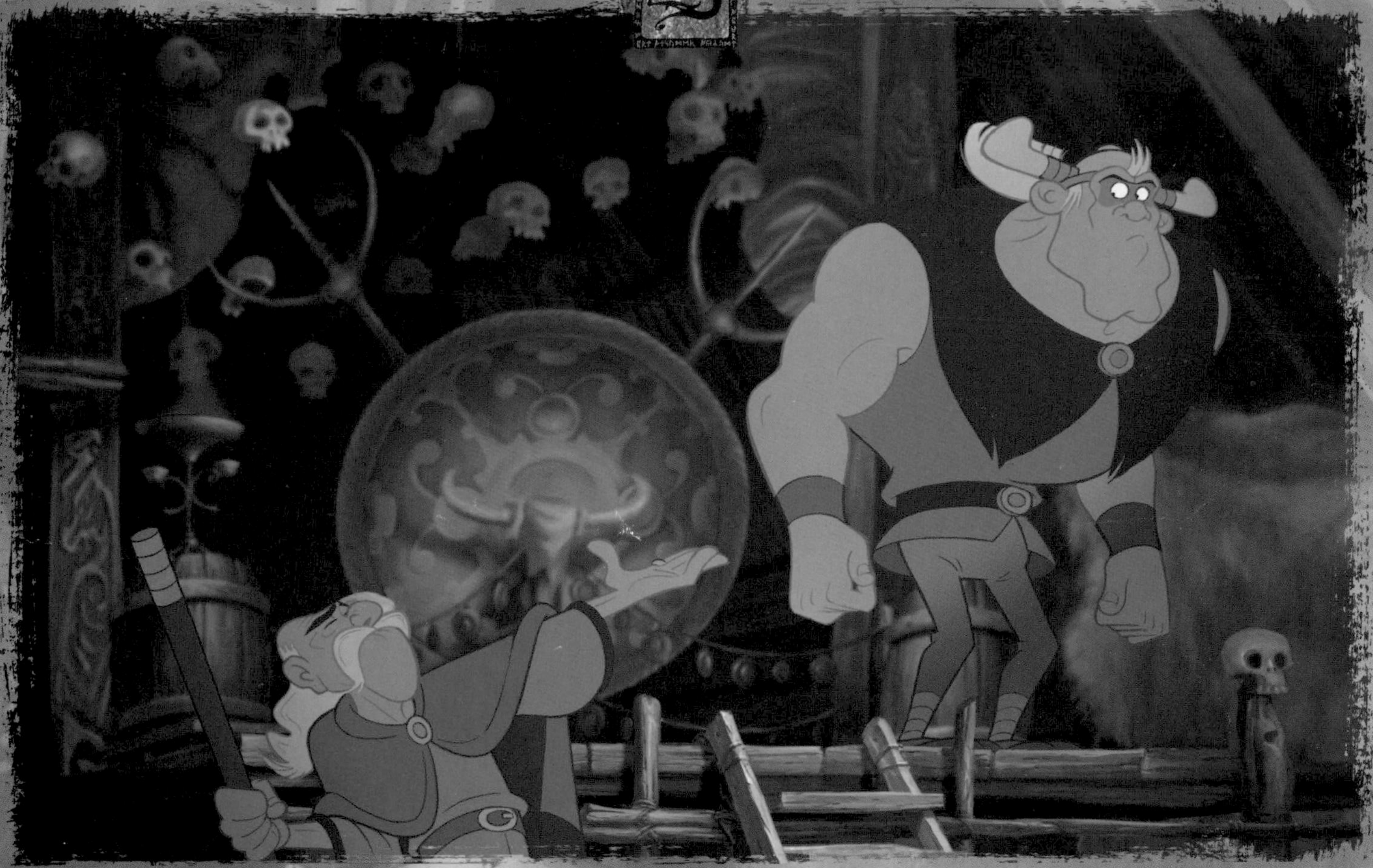

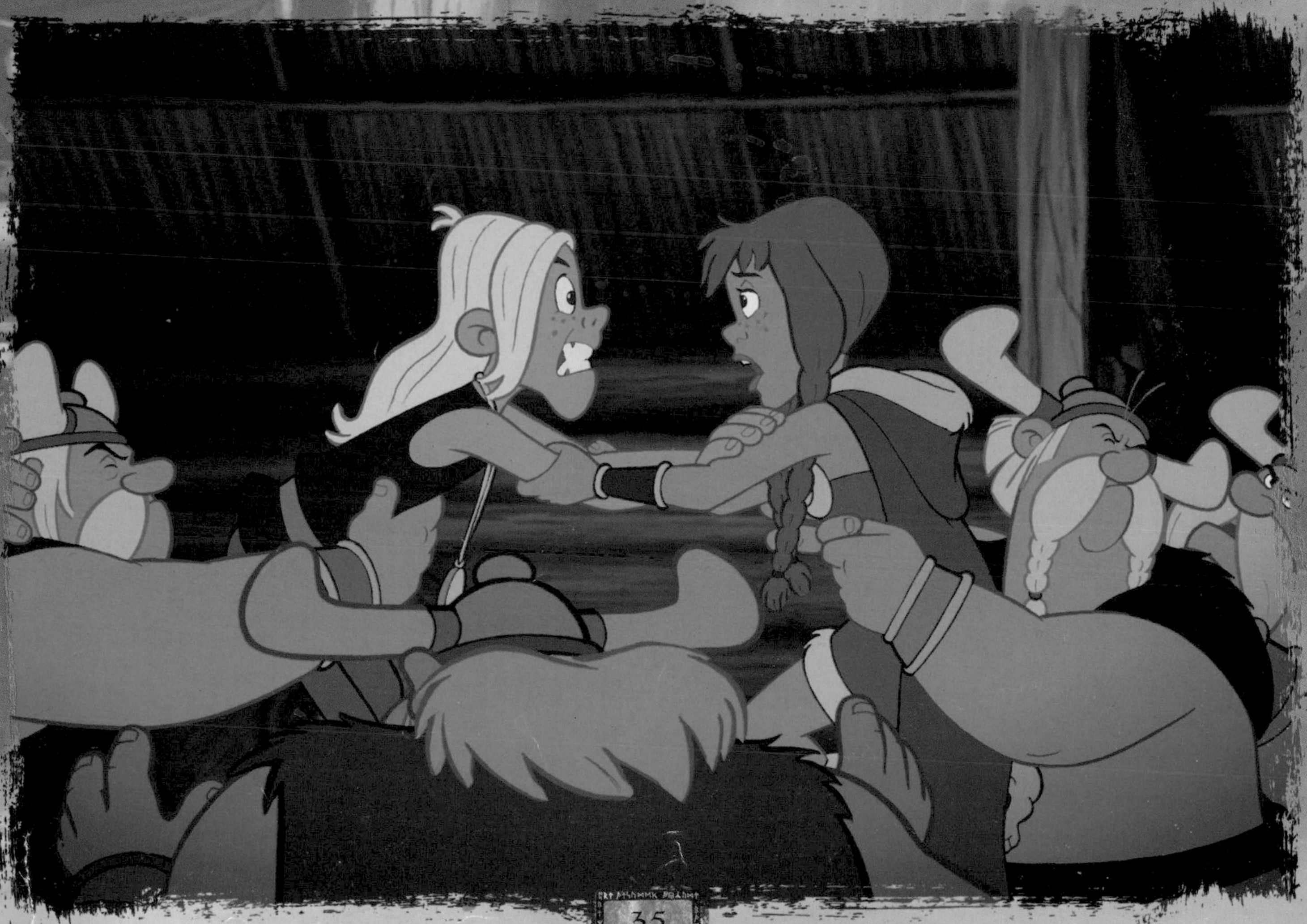

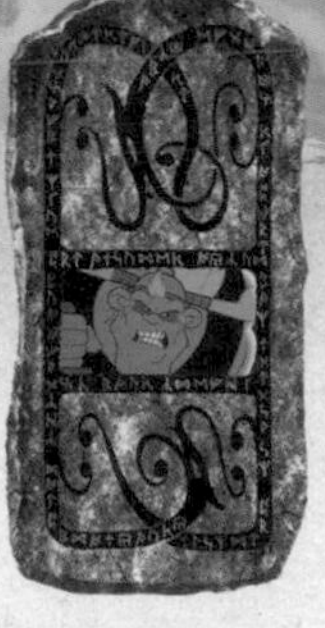

Outside, Obelix is walking through the night, his feet sinking deep into the snow. A doorman goes flying, a house collapses – in his wounded pride, he flattens everything in sight like a steamroller. Even the snowflakes seem heavy-hearted. Asterix tries to catch up with his friend and persuade him that they must go back and help Justforkix.

But Obelix marches straight ahead over a suspension bridge. All Asterix's arguments are in vain. Only the faithful Dogmatix deserves his friendship, thinks Obelix, and he never wants to hear about Justforkix again. 'Help the boy? After those things he said? Impossible,' he says.

But now Asterix finds the argument that will change his mind. 'Did you say impossible? That's what Justforkix said when you told him to pick up the menhir! You mean there's something you can't do?'

The mere suggestion is an insult that goes home, making Obelix forget Justforkix's harsh words. He turns and retraces his steps. Our friends go back to the Viking village together, on their way to rescue Justforkix and save the honour of their little Armorican village.

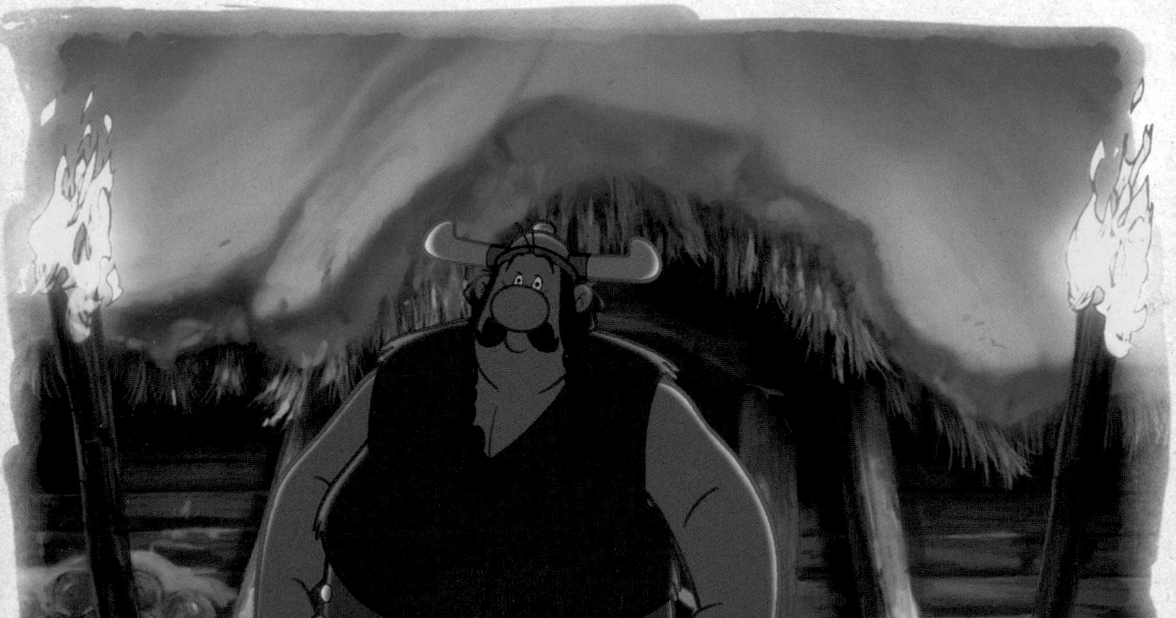

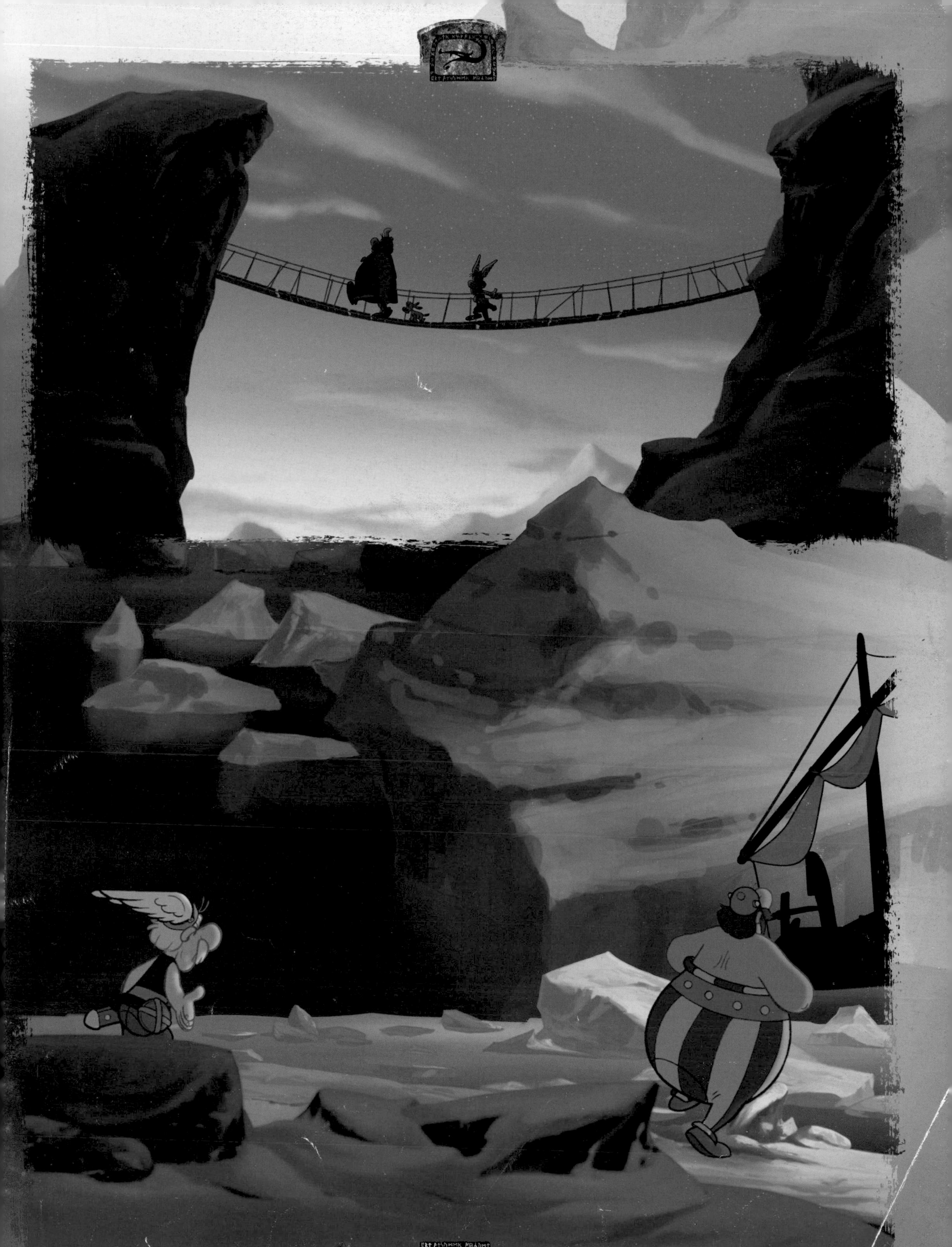

Viking roosters greet the dawn with loud crowing, like the Gaulish variety. And the wake-up call that sends you flying through the window seems to be a custom all over the world. National differences depend only on whether you land on straw, dunghills, beaten earth … or, in this case, snow.

Now the day can begin.

'Go on,' Timandahaf tells his Gaulish captive. 'Frighten us!'

This means life or death to Justforkix. He remembers his boyhood in Lutetia, when he and the other street urchins used to compete in making faces. He pulls some faces. He might as well have tried tickling an elephant with a feather. He utters a faint growl.

'What's all this nonsense?' says Timandahaf. 'Now this is what I call a terrifying yell … WOOOAH!'

'Eeek!'

All any Viking has to do to scare Justforkix silly is open his mouth. Timandahaf is getting tired of such a feeble performance. 'That's enough chit-chat!' he says. 'Let's have your flying demonstration. Off we go to get you on the runway!'

'No! No!'

So when Asterix and Obelix reach the Viking village, there's no one around. Only a single Viking buried headfirst in the snow. Asterix takes him out and smacks his face.

'Are you or aren't you going to talk? Yes or no?'

'No! Viking … fly!'

And he does, too, when Asterix sends him sailing through the air.

Justforkix is standing on top of the cliff, with a steep drop below him. His teeth are chattering. This wasn't in Cryptograf's plan, and now he's trying to gain time. Quickly, he slips a rope round the young man's waist, just before he's thrown off the top of the cliff … and guess what? Justforkix is flying!

The delighted Vikings, with Timandahaf in the lead, run to the edge of the cliff ready to throw themselves off too.

'STOP! Let's have the wedding first,' Cryptograf reminds them.

Brought up short at the last minute, they turn round, leaving young Justforkix dangling.

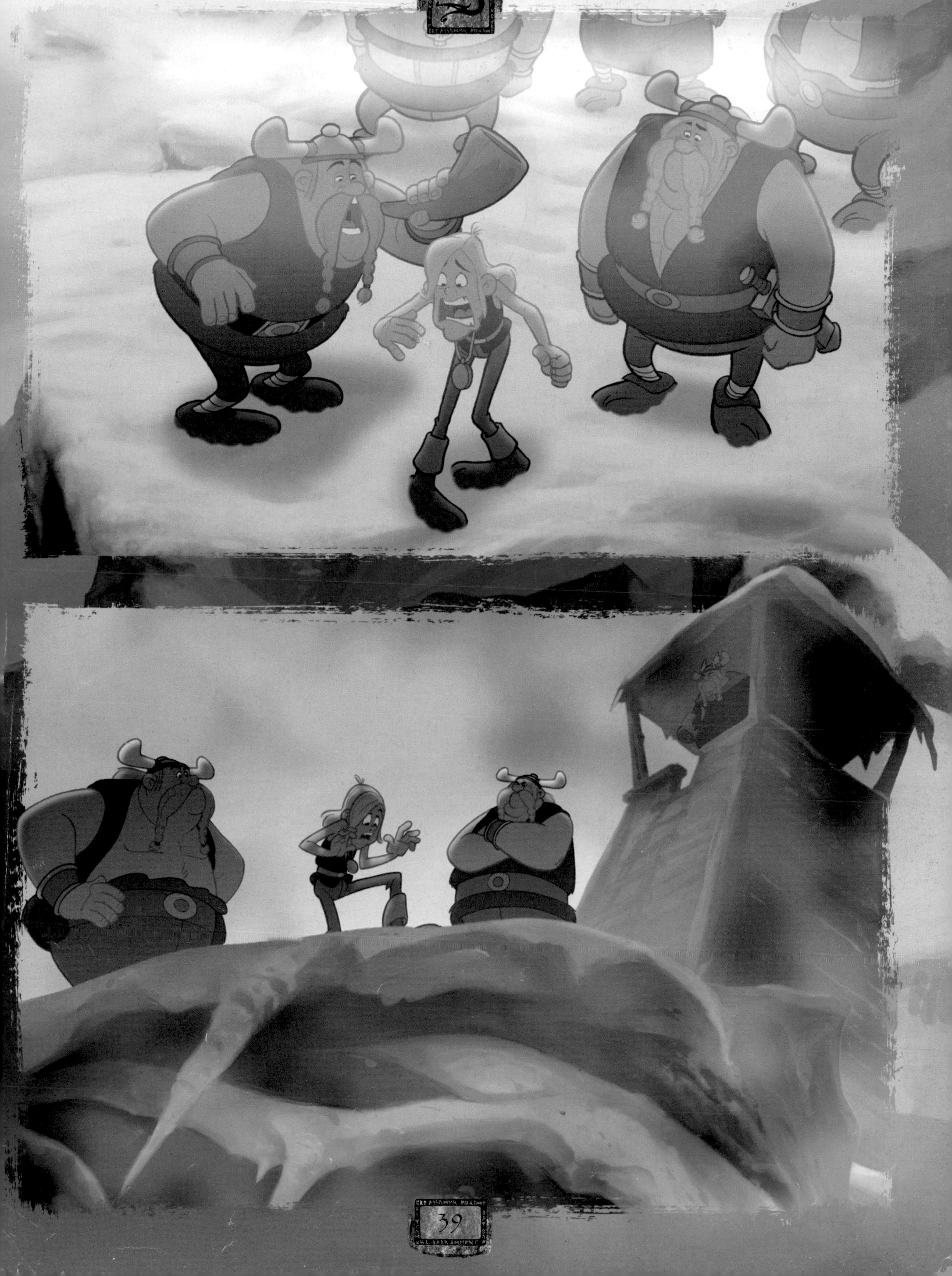

Alone in space, Justforkix really does seem to be flying. He can't go forward or back, he's been liberated from the law of gravity, he's hovering. But higher up, on top of a control tower, Olaf looks as if he's fishing. He is holding a rod, and now, as the mist drifts aside, anyone can see that the fishing line is the other end of the rope round Justforkix's waist.

So that's how the trick was done! And Cryptograf, also balancing on the roof of the control tower, begins cutting through the rope to get rid of the champion of fear, who has now served his purpose. But before the soothsayer has quite finished cutting, he slips in the snow. Justforkix's life is literally dangling by a thread.

And crash! As the thread breaks, Justforkix plunges into the abyss. SMS dives with him. As if they were a circus act, Justforkix catches her feet, hanging from the bird – and once again he seems to be flying, caught in mid-air by the Gauls who have turned up to save him in the nick of time.

He flings himself on Obelix's broad chest, and then hugs Asterix. All is forgotten and forgiven.

'Time to go home,' says Asterix.

'No!' And Justforkix explains. 'We must rescue Abba. She needs me.'

'Nothing doing! We're going home now.'

How selfish young folk can be! Forgetting his gratitude and their emotional reunion just a moment ago, Justforkix turns against the Gauls again, hammering Obelix on the back with his fists.

Meanwhile Abba, with her hands tied, is struggling frantically as Olaf hauls her away under the eyes of his parents. This is their son's wedding day, and they are deeply moved.

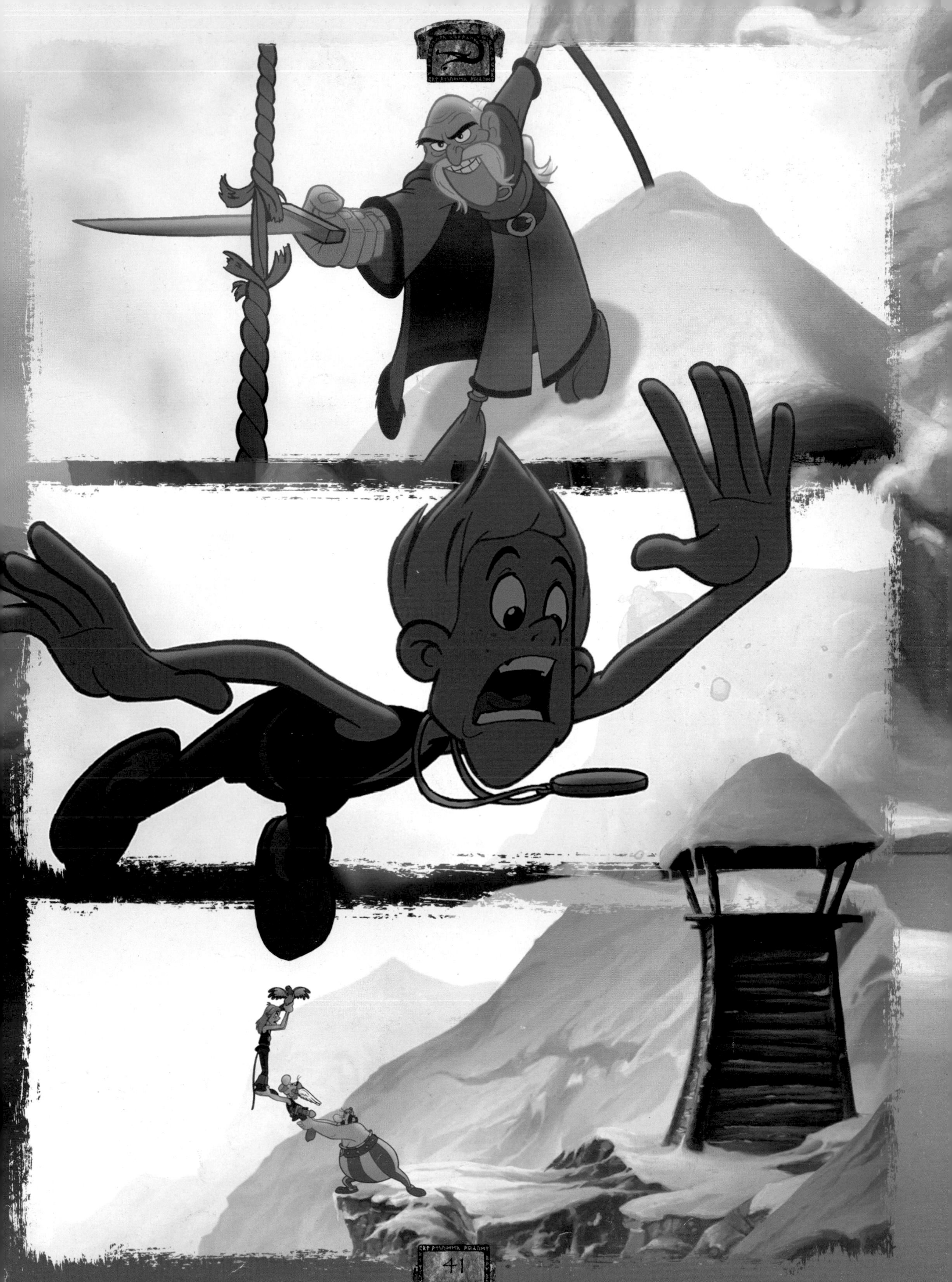

While the Gauls make for their ship, moored at the entrance to the fjord, and go aboard, Justforkix is still arguing. At last Obelix's heart is softened.

'Oh, why don't we go and look for the little Viking girl, Asterix?' he asks. 'It will make young Justforkix so happy!'

'Nothing doing!' says Asterix.

Once again the two friends' educational theories are at odds. But when the young man spots the gourd of magic potion at Asterix's belt, he doesn't hesitate to help himself to some.

So as they carry on arguing, silhouetted against the snow, Justforkix, all tanked up on potion, jumps ship and swims strongly back to the village.

Abba is still resisting the marriage as hard as she can, but her own parents too watch the traditional ceremony with sentimental pleasure.

'You just wait till Justforkix gets back!' she threatens.

Cryptograf laughs heartily. He's sure the young man has fallen to the bottom of the cliff and will never be seen again. But suddenly …

'Nobody move! The wedding's off!'

And in true Viking tradition, Justforkix flings the girl over his shoulder and carries her away. The non-traditional bit is that she's willing, even delighted!

A general punch-up follows. When Asterix and Obelix turn up to rescue the young people, Asterix takes a good swig of potion himself and goes into action. Meanwhile, the lovers take advantage of the brawl to run away in the snow and reach the Gaulish ship.

Seeing political power escape his grasp, Cryptograf gives his son a simple order: kill the champion. Olaf understands that, no problem, and he sets off after them with all the strength and determination of a man who can entertain only one idea at a time.

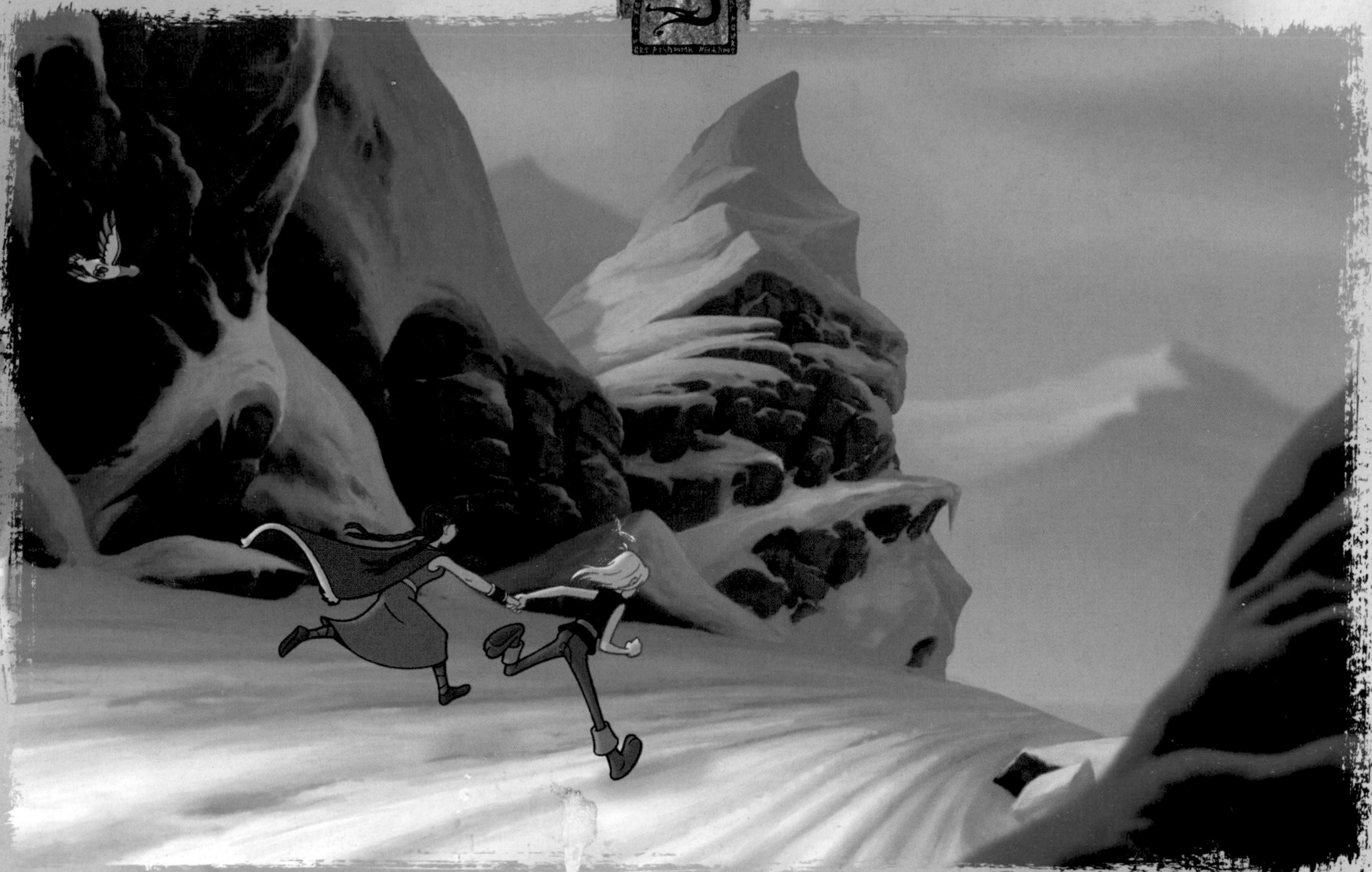

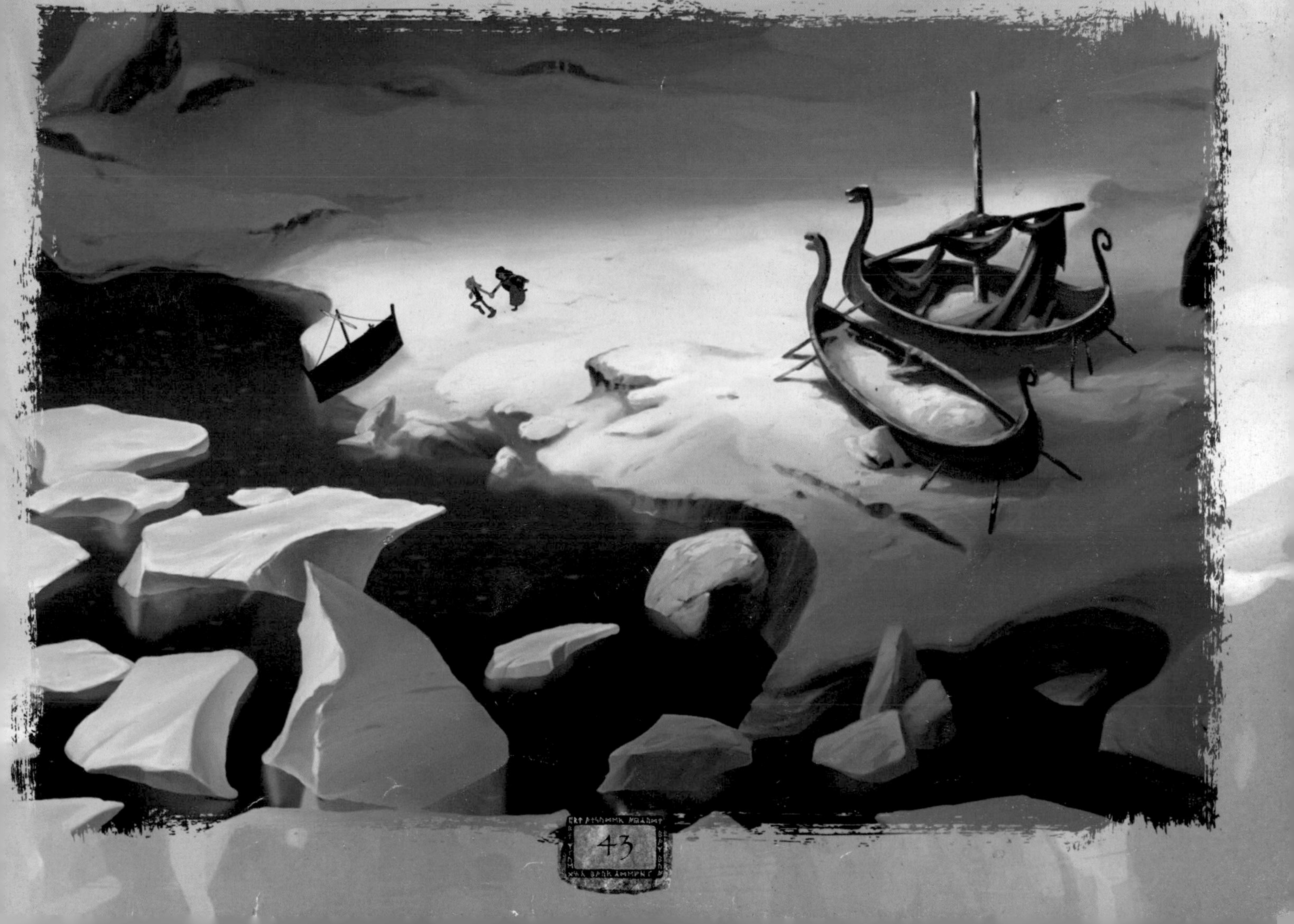

The young couple are just going on board the ship when they see Olaf, taking gigantic strides as he leaps from ice floe to ice floe. Justforkix picks up an oar and threatens to snap it, to show Olaf how strong he is. But the effects of the magic potion have worn off, and it resists his puny strength. Meanwhile Olaf has grabbed the boom of the sail. Seeing that Justforkix is terrified again, Abba says encouragingly, 'Go on, fly away! I'll fly too, in your arms!'

Feeling ashamed of himself, Justforkix finally admits that he can't fly at all.

'What?' cries Abba. 'You're no better than anyone else! You lied to me!'

Poor Justforkix has to fight on all fronts now, trying to fend off the brutal Olaf with his oar and at the same time stop his beloved Abba leaving.

'I didn't want to lie to you,' he tells her. 'I had to, in spite of myself.'

Meanwhile SMS is flying off to warn Asterix and Obelix, but the dove is exhausted on reaching them, and unable to pass on any message. A quick drink of potion, however, gives her new energy to peck the message out on the ice. What a beak! They follow SMS back to the fjord.

Out there matters are worse than ever. Deaf to the pleas of Justforkix, Abba leaves her two suitors to their fate. But when Olaf seizes Justforkix, who lets out a scream, she turns back and shouts, 'No! No! Don't kill him!'

In all the scuffling, however, she's the one who is knocked senseless. The two rivals are facing each other not far from a steaming crater now. Justforkix realises that it is a geyser, and could come in useful – sure enough, when Olaf falls into it, it erupts and flings him up in the air to land a long way off. By the time Asterix and Obelix arrive, followed by a Viking horde, Abba is coming round.

Timandahaf gives his men orders to capture Justforkix before he can fly away. This time all is revealed. Justforkix is a liar and can't fly at all. Olaf was holding him up in the air by a rope – 'Right, Dad?' he appeals. And the sly Cryptograf fixed the whole thing. His plot is uncovered, and all he can say in self-defence is that Odin must have lied to him!

A dramatic scene unfolds on the icy cliffs. Cryptograf slides towards the abyss below, clinging to Abba's cloak. Justforkix catches hold of her just in time, and they reach a ledge on the side of the cliff, exactly where the boom fell after Olaf dropped it. Asterix shouts to them not to move, and he and Obelix will come for them. But how? 'This is the end,' says Abba, and she's right. 'Flying is the only way to get out of here – and that's impossible!'

'Impossible? Doesn't that remind you of something?' Justforkix remembers now. 'A very good friend once told me, how do you know something's impossible until you try?'

Asterix and Obelix shout, 'No!'

But too late …

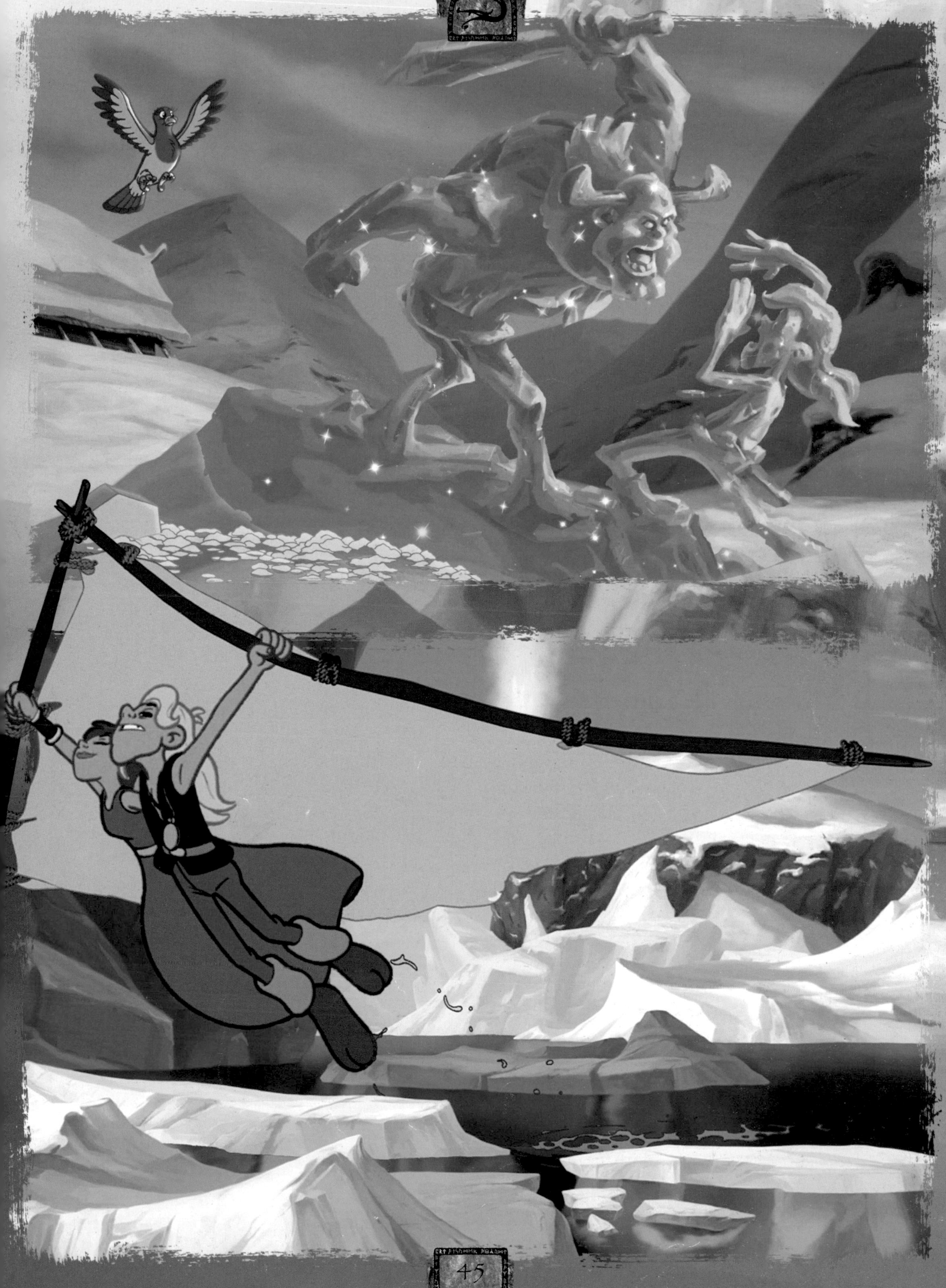

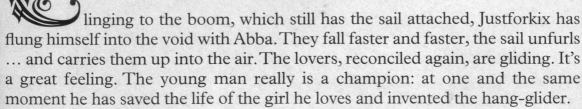

Clinging to the boom, which still has the sail attached, Justforkix has flung himself into the void with Abba. They fall faster and faster, the sail unfurls … and carries them up into the air. The lovers, reconciled again, are gliding. It's a great feeling. The young man really is a champion: at one and the same moment he has saved the life of the girl he loves and invented the hang-glider.

His personal trainers are astonished. He really is doing very well.

'You see, Obelix,' says Asterix, 'it's love, not fear, that lends you wings!'

Cryptograf could do with something to lend *him* wings, clinging as he is to the cliffside. Oh for a little love to get him out of there!

At the next full moon, as he promised, Doublehelix is back in the village. But there is no sign of Justforkix yet.

'Er, I think he's gone hunting … er, fishing,' Vitalstatistix says.

'Hunting or fishing, which is it? Make up your mind!'

While our heroes are doing their best to get home in time, the villagers keep Doublehelix happy with plenty of boar, barley beer and hopeful attempts to explain. But things look bad – until in the nick of time Justforkix turns up, with Abba in his arms.

The marriage between the young people is about to take place. The Vikings in their longship have followed Asterix, Obelix and Justforkix all the way back from the frozen North, but now they join the Gauls to celebrate the wedding in the village of the indomitable Gauls. The Viking wedding guests tell the tale of Justforkix's many adventures, and Doublehelix feels very proud of his son.

Asterix turns to the druid Getafix. 'Tell me, Getafix, how would you define fear?'

'Fear is a test of courage,' says the druid. 'True courage means overcoming your fear.'

At this point the bard speaks up. 'I will now give you an ode in celebration of this happy event.' And he plucks the strings of his lyre, chanting tunelessly, 'Lurve … it's lurve that makes the ancient wuurrrld go round!'

The Vikings are transfixed by terror. They clutch their heads, making frightful faces.

'What's this barbaric noise? It's unbearable!'

'By Thor! By Odin! Bye-bye!'

And they flee for their lives, swimming out to their ship, suddenly very keen to get away from the bard and back home to the frozen North.

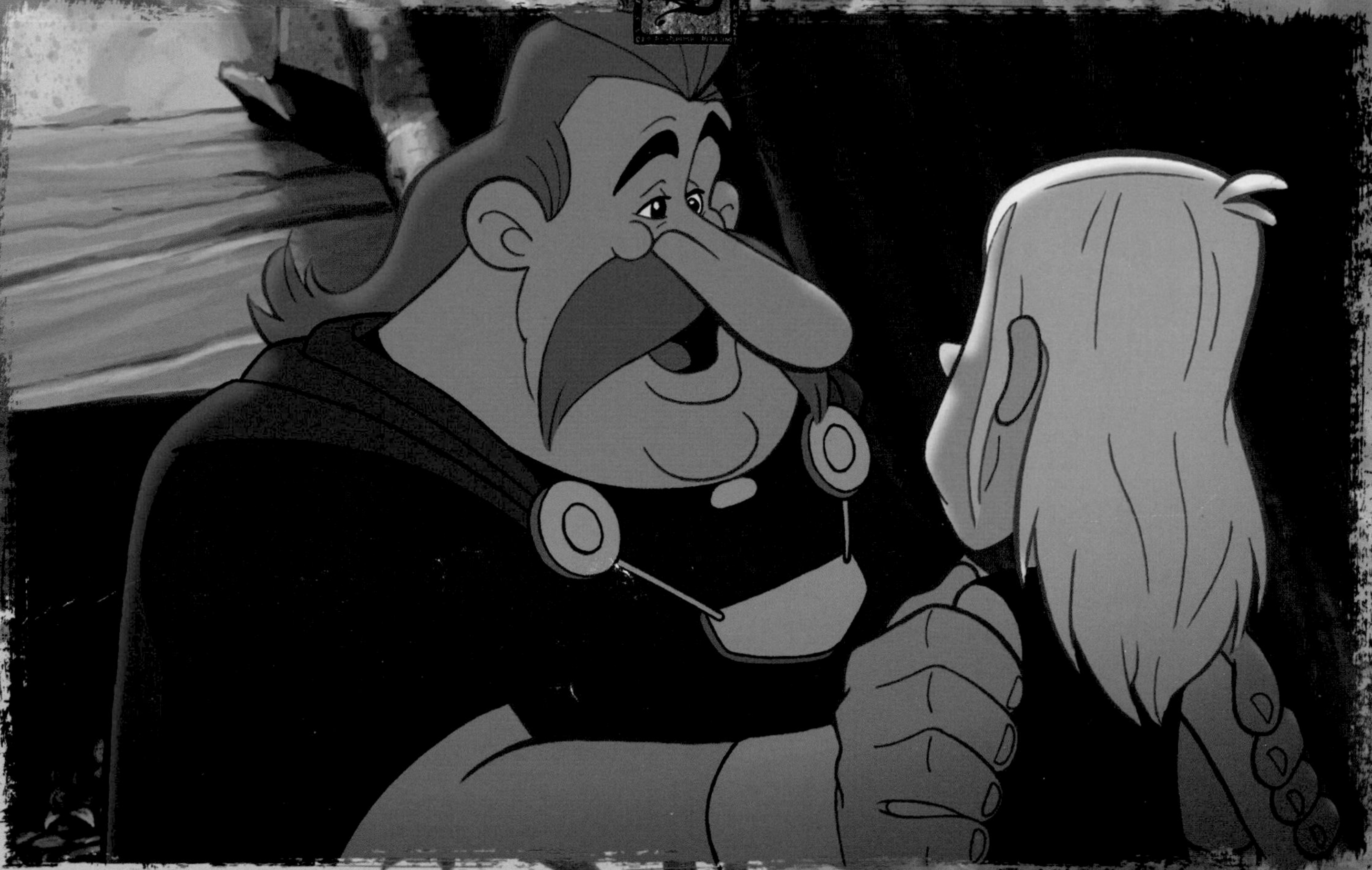

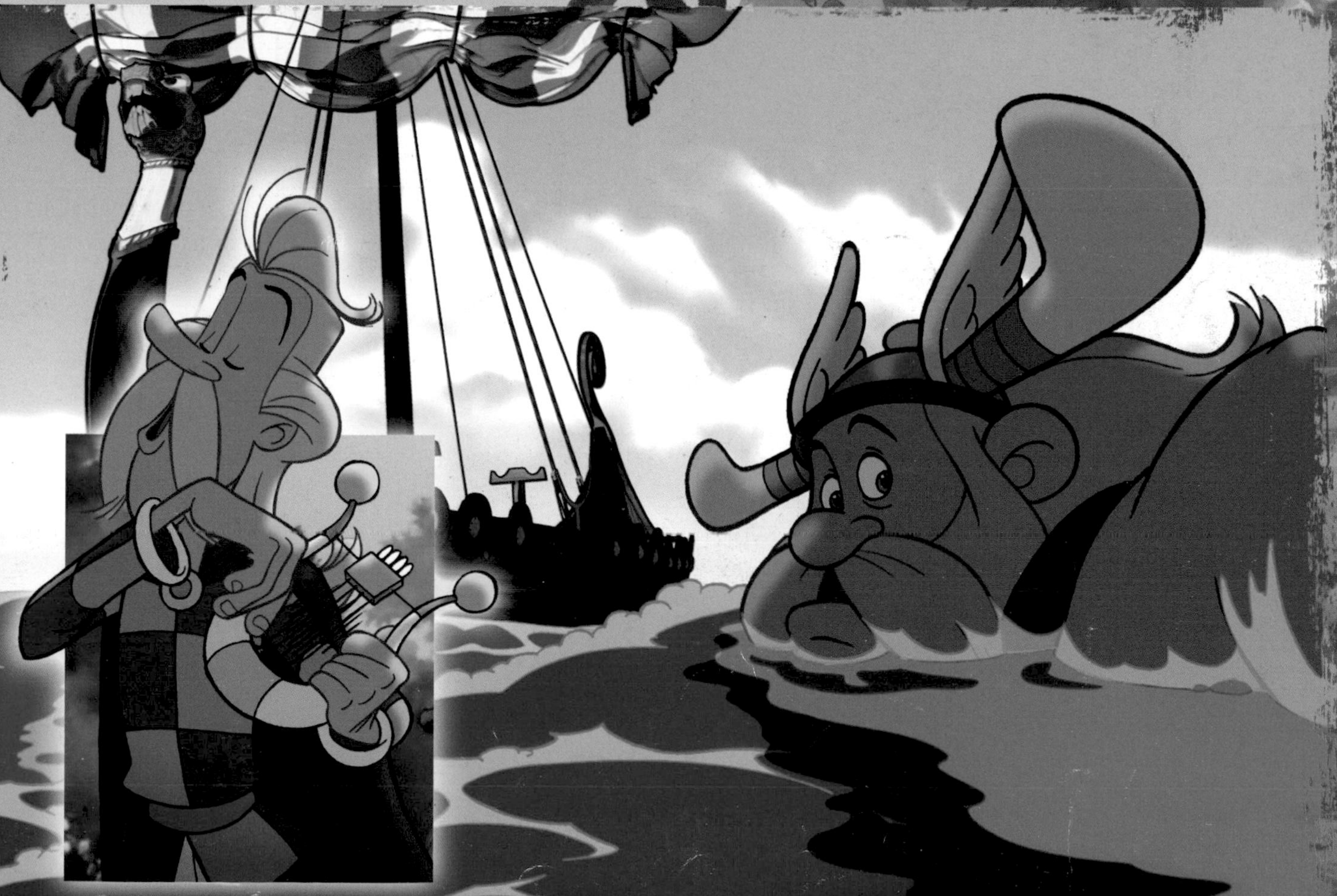

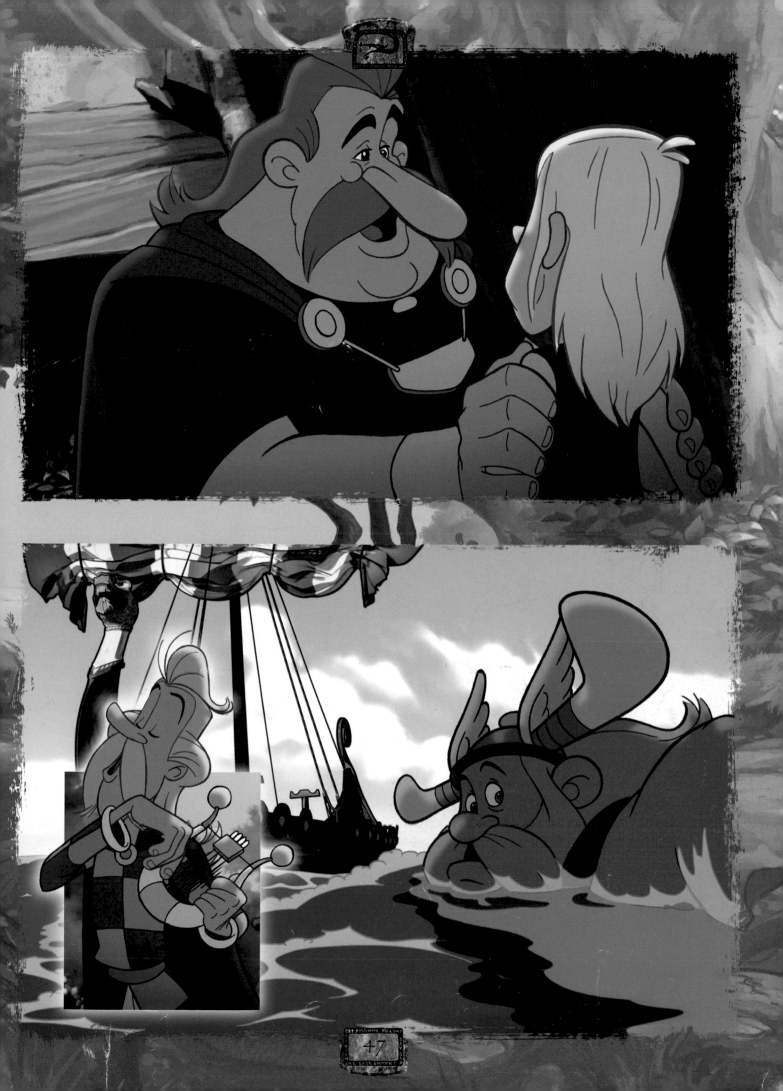

As for the Gauls, enjoying their traditional banquet, they celebrate the great deeds of Justforkix, his young wife, Asterix and Obelix … and spare a thought for their new friends the Vikings, who will now sail the seas in a constant state of fear and trembling.

THE END

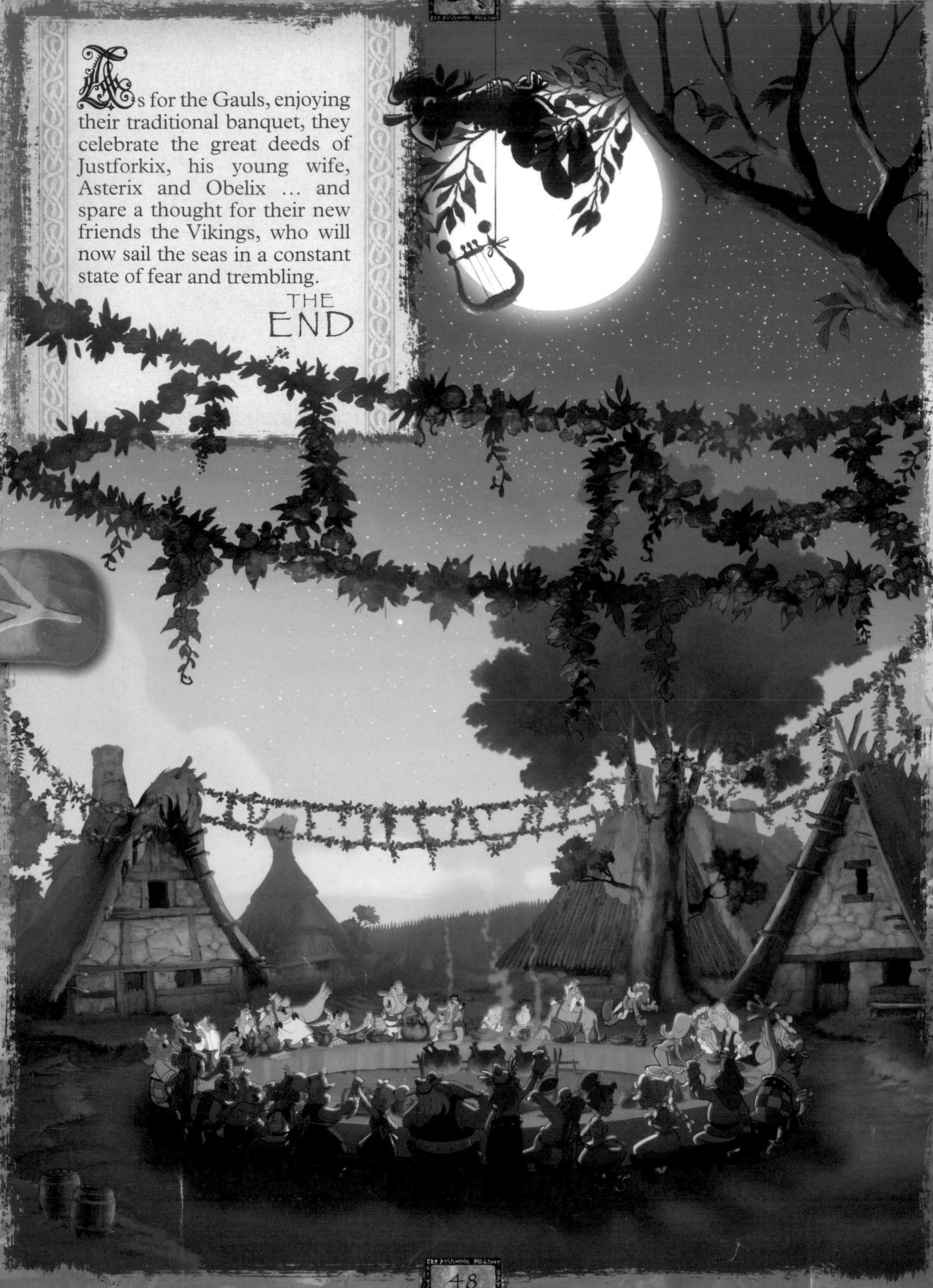

HOW
THIS FILM
WAS MADE

BY DOUBLECLIX

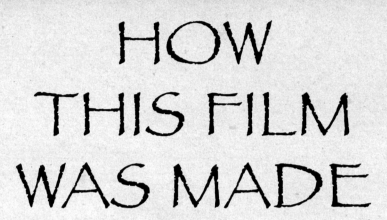

subtle
stuff!

no
comments,

ASTERIX FS INSPIRATIONAL 01 031114

ASTERIX MODEL
CORRECTIONS TRACED BY ALBERT UDERZO

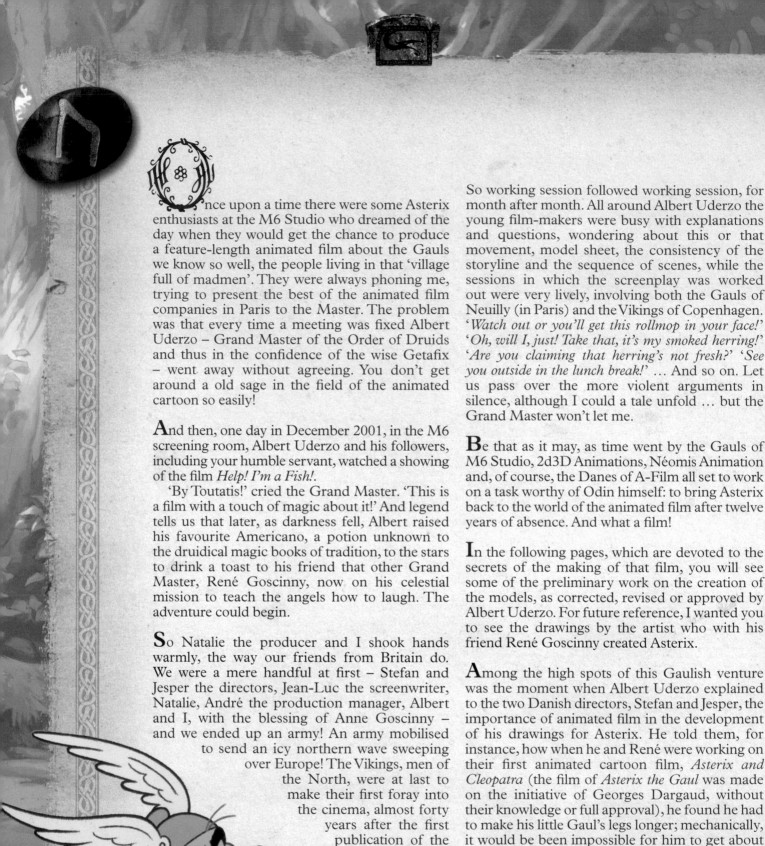

Once upon a time there were some Asterix enthusiasts at the M6 Studio who dreamed of the day when they would get the chance to produce a feature-length animated film about the Gauls we know so well, the people living in that 'village full of madmen'. They were always phoning me, trying to present the best of the animated film companies in Paris to the Master. The problem was that every time a meeting was fixed Albert Uderzo – Grand Master of the Order of Druids and thus in the confidence of the wise Getafix – went away without agreeing. You don't get around a old sage in the field of the animated cartoon so easily!

And then, one day in December 2001, in the M6 screening room, Albert Uderzo and his followers, including your humble servant, watched a showing of the film *Help! I'm a Fish!*.

'By Toutatis!' cried the Grand Master. 'This is a film with a touch of magic about it!' And legend tells us that later, as darkness fell, Albert raised his favourite Americano, a potion unknown to the druidical magic books of tradition, to the stars to drink a toast to his friend that other Grand Master, René Goscinny, now on his celestial mission to teach the angels how to laugh. The adventure could begin.

So Natalie the producer and I shook hands warmly, the way our friends from Britain do. We were a mere handful at first – Stefan and Jesper the directors, Jean-Luc the screenwriter, Natalie, André the production manager, Albert and I, with the blessing of Anne Goscinny – and we ended up an army! An army mobilised to send an icy northern wave sweeping over Europe! The Vikings, men of the North, were at last to make their first foray into the cinema, almost forty years after the first publication of the album *Asterix and the Normans*. You will remember that they wanted to learn how to feel fear, because of course fear lends you wings!

So working session followed working session, for month after month. All around Albert Uderzo the young film-makers were busy with explanations and questions, wondering about this or that movement, model sheet, the consistency of the storyline and the sequence of scenes, while the sessions in which the screenplay was worked out were very lively, involving both the Gauls of Neuilly (in Paris) and the Vikings of Copenhagen. '*Watch out or you'll get this rollmop in your face!*' '*Oh, will I, just! Take that, it's my smoked herring!*' '*Are you claiming that herring's not fresh?*' '*See you outside in the lunch break!*' … And so on. Let us pass over the more violent arguments in silence, although I could a tale unfold … but the Grand Master won't let me.

Be that as it may, as time went by the Gauls of M6 Studio, 2d3D Animations, Néomis Animation and, of course, the Danes of A-Film all set to work on a task worthy of Odin himself: to bring Asterix back to the world of the animated film after twelve years of absence. And what a film!

In the following pages, which are devoted to the secrets of the making of that film, you will see some of the preliminary work on the creation of the models, as corrected, revised or approved by Albert Uderzo. For future reference, I wanted you to see the drawings by the artist who with his friend René Goscinny created Asterix.

Among the high spots of this Gaulish venture was the moment when Albert Uderzo explained to the two Danish directors, Stefan and Jesper, the importance of animated film in the development of his drawings for Asterix. He told them, for instance, how when he and René were working on their first animated cartoon film, *Asterix and Cleopatra* (the film of *Asterix the Gaul* was made on the initiative of Georges Dargaud, without their knowledge or full approval), he found he had to make his little Gaul's legs longer; mechanically, it would be been impossible for him to get about normally with the short legs shown in the very first strip-cartoon albums.

So enjoy your journey to the country imagined by Goscinny and Uderzo, a land that has been offering the joys of escapism to generations of readers ever since 1959. For after all, it's imagination that really lends us wings, wouldn't you agree?

Doubleclix

HEAD OF ASTERIX, MODEL SHEET
CORRECTIONS TRACED BY ALBERT UDERZO

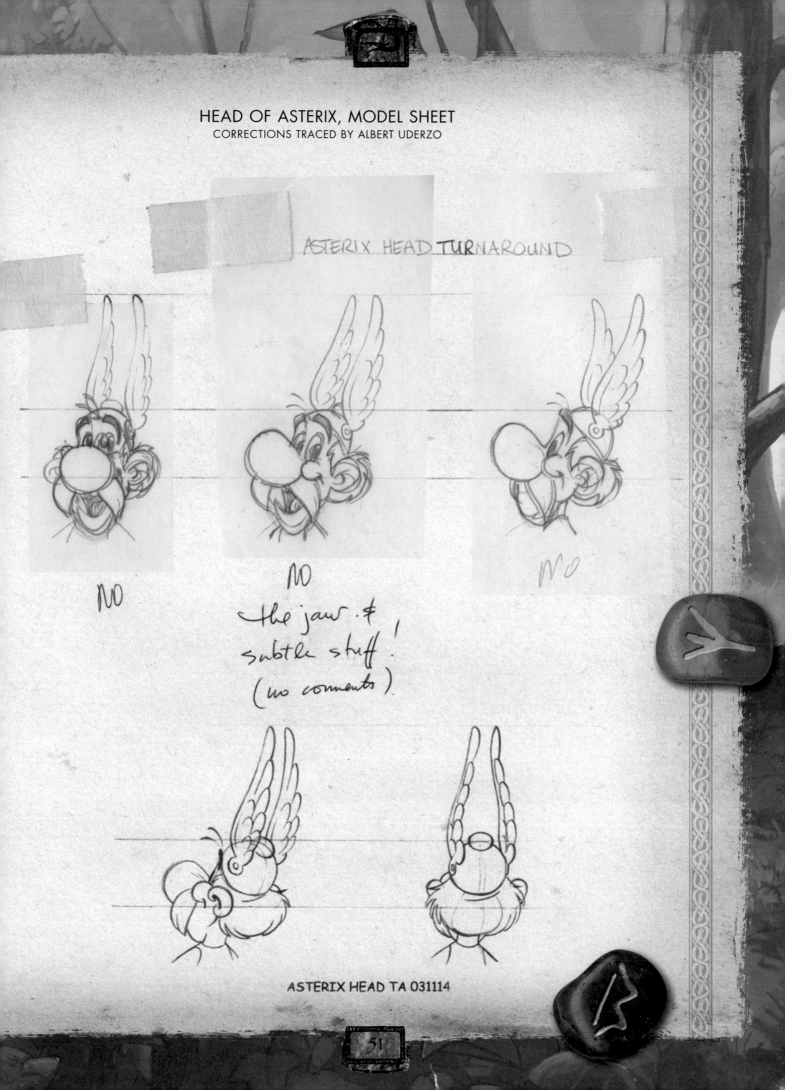

ASTERIX HEAD TURNAROUND

NO

NO

NO

the jaw .&
subtle stuff !
(no comments)

ASTERIX HEAD TA 031114

PRELIMINARY WORK FOR TIMANDAHAF'S HOUSE

Source: M6 Studio

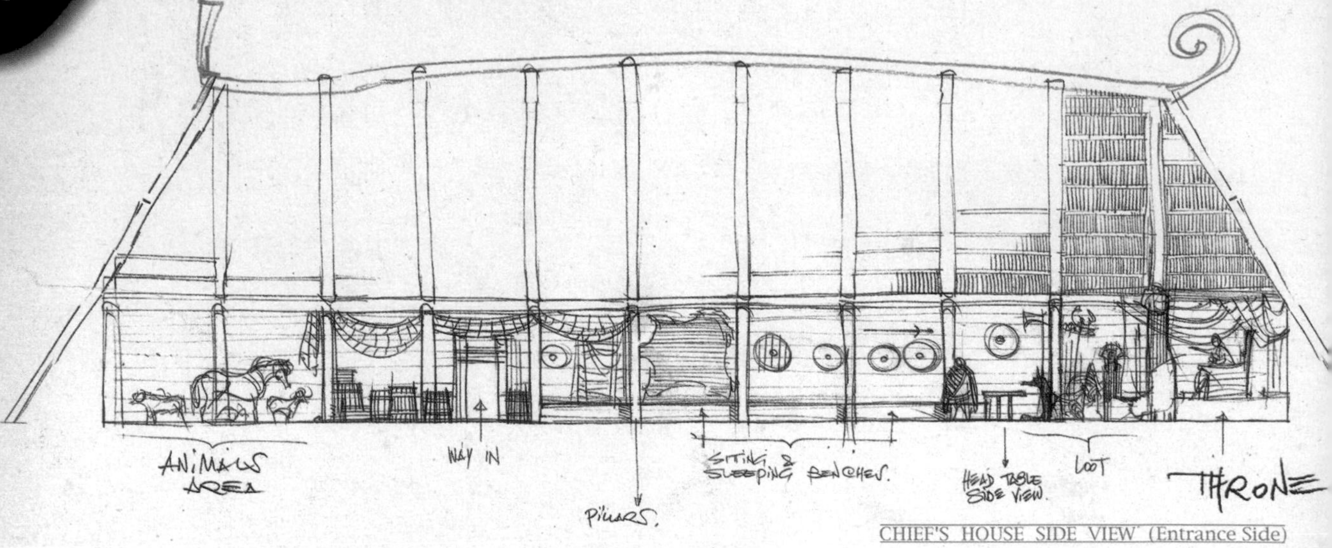

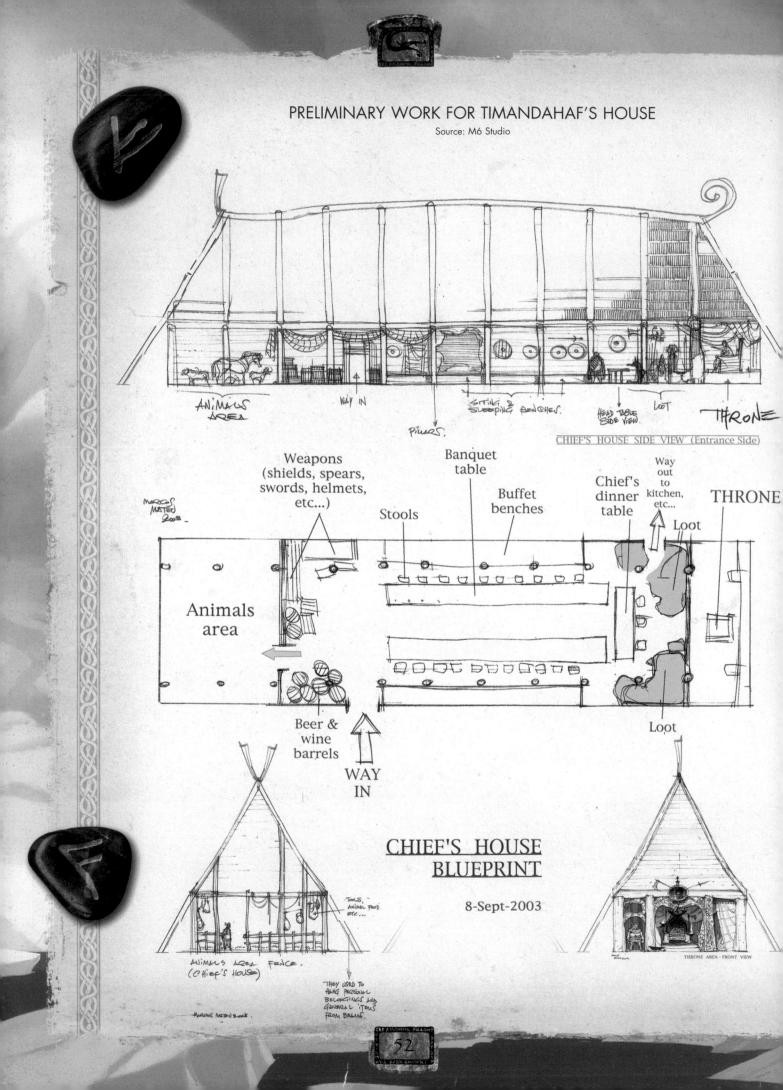

ANIMALS AREA
WAY IN
PILLARS.
SITTING & SLEEPING BENCHES.
HEAD TABLE SIDE VIEW.
LOOT
THRONE

CHIEF'S HOUSE SIDE VIEW (Entrance Side)

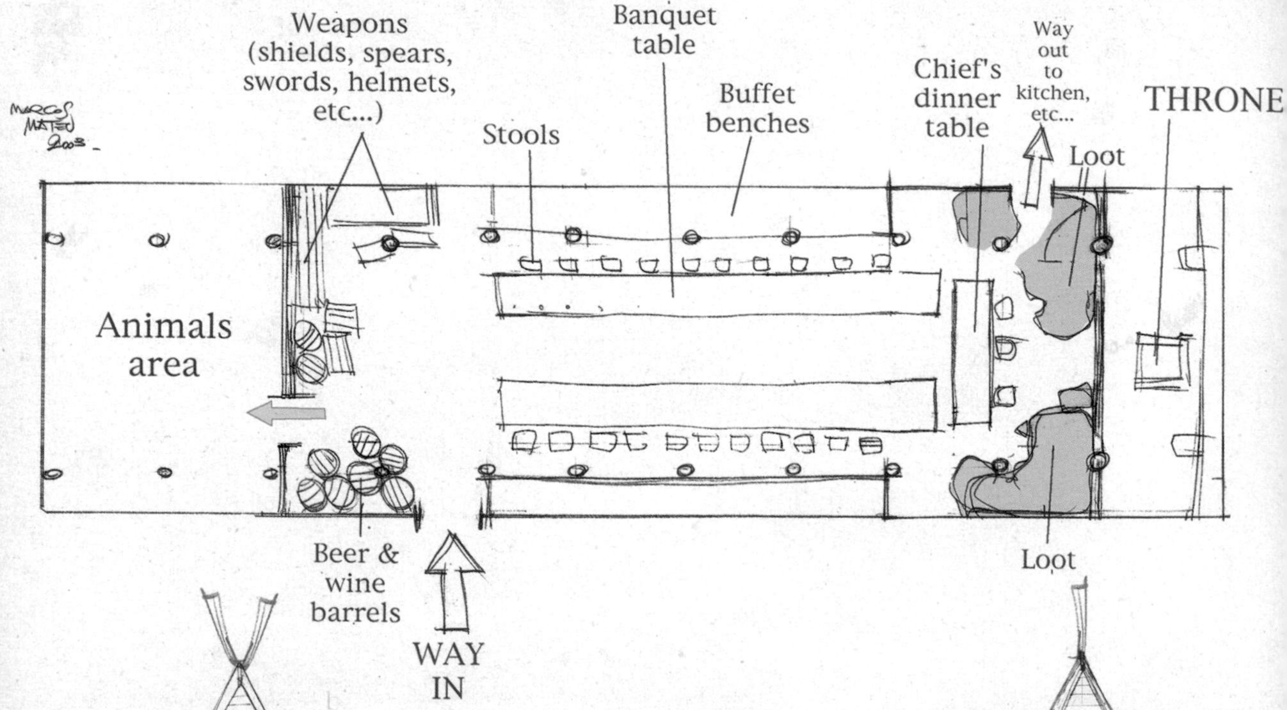

MARCOS MATEU 2003
Weapons (shields, spears, swords, helmets, etc...)
Banquet table
Buffet benches
Stools
Chief's dinner table
Way out to kitchen, etc...
THRONE
Loot
Animals area
Beer & wine barrels
WAY IN
Loot

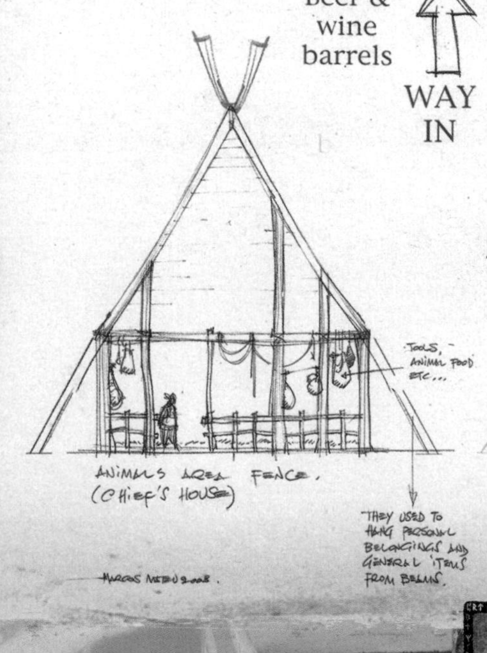

TOOLS, ANIMAL FOOD ETC...
ANIMALS AREA FENCE. (CHIEF'S HOUSE)
THEY USED TO HANG PERSONAL BELONGINGS AND GENERAL ITEMS FROM BEAMS.
MARCOS MATEU 2003

CHIEF'S HOUSE BLUEPRINT

8-Sept-2003

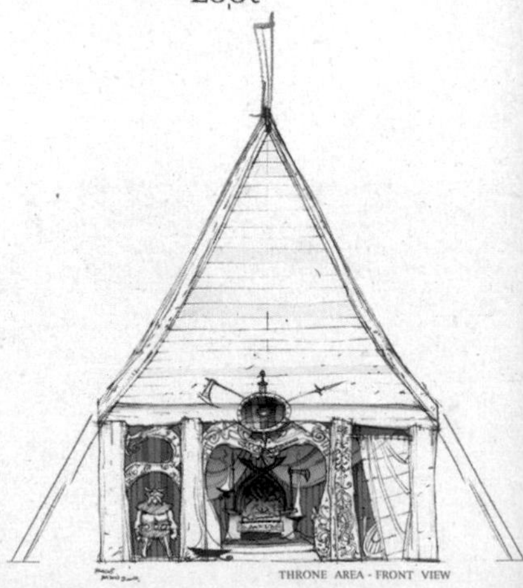

THRONE AREA - FRONT VIEW

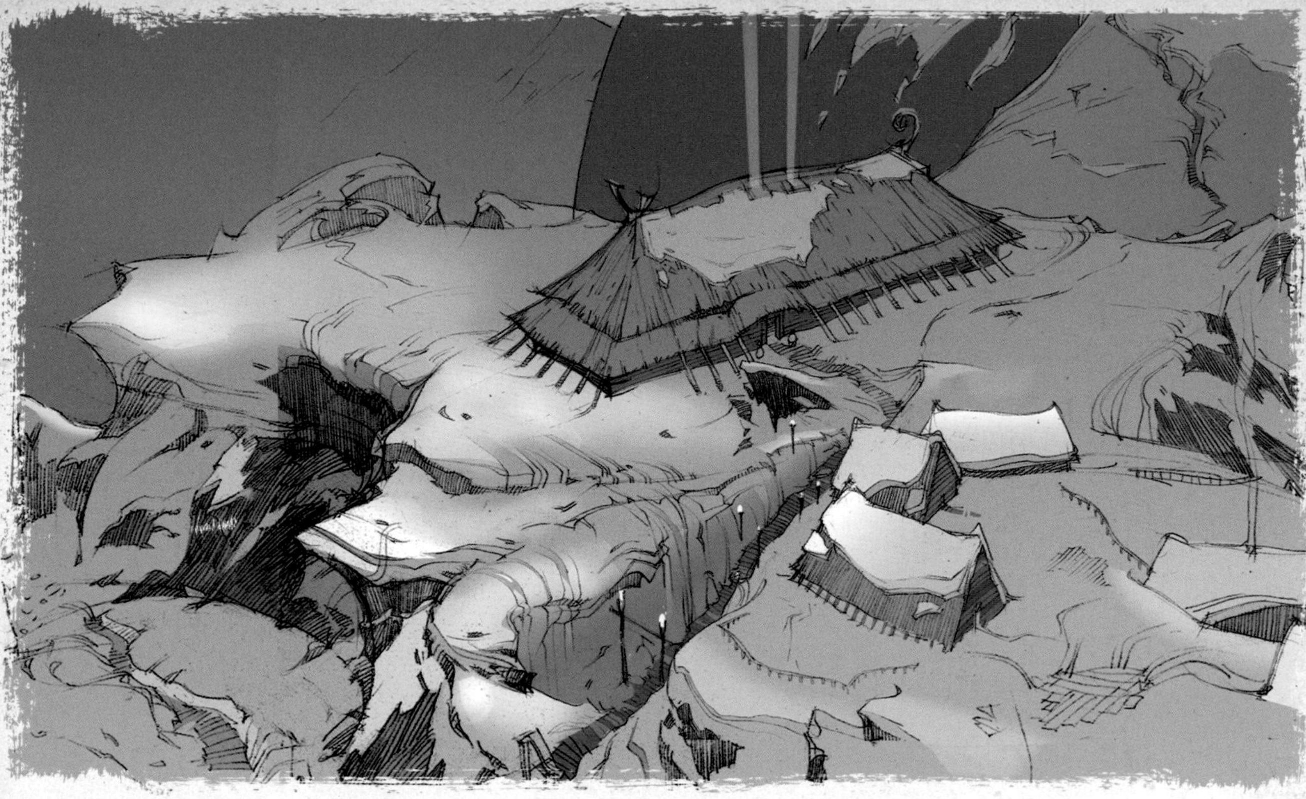

OUTDOOR SCENE AND BANQUETING HALL

Source: M6 Studio

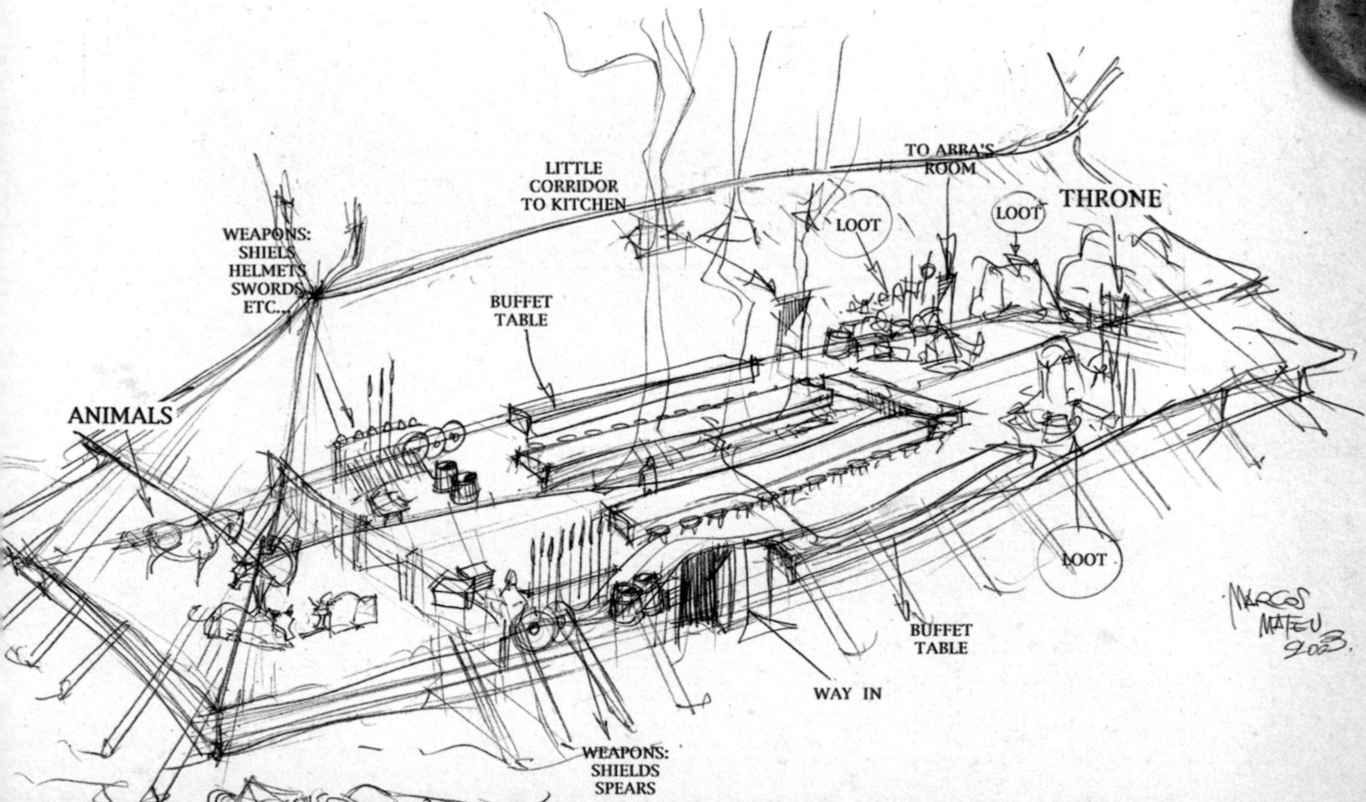
LITTLE
CORRIDOR
TO KITCHEN
TO ABBA'S
ROOM
THRONE
LOOT
LOOT
WEAPONS:
SHIELS
HELMETS
SWORDS
ETC...
BUFFET
TABLE
ANIMALS
LOOT
BUFFET
TABLE
WAY IN
WEAPONS:
SHIELDS
SPEARS
MARCOS
MATEU
2003.

CACOFONIX FX 01 031114

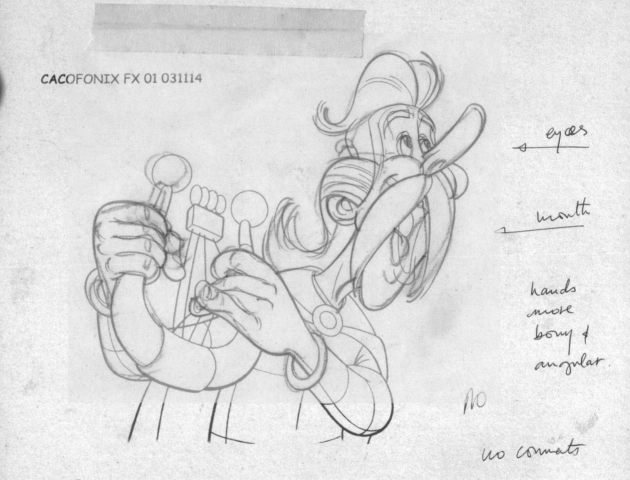

eyes

mouth

hands
more
bony &
angular.

no

no comments

legs a bit longer   CACOFONIX FS TA 031114

no

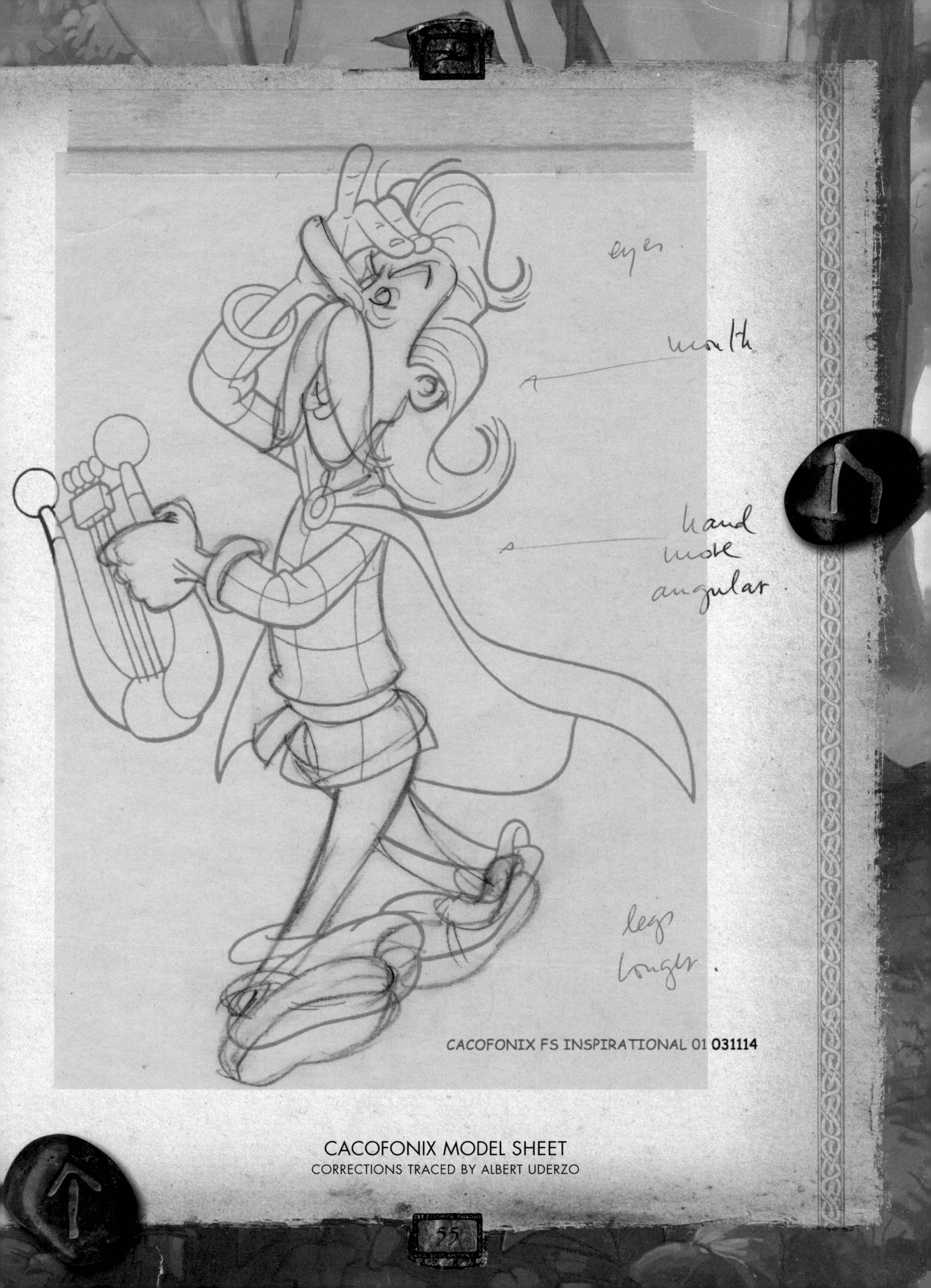
eyes
mouth
hand more angular.
legs longer.
CACOFONIX FS INSPIRATIONAL 01 031114

CACOFONIX MODEL SHEET
CORRECTIONS TRACED BY ALBERT UDERZO

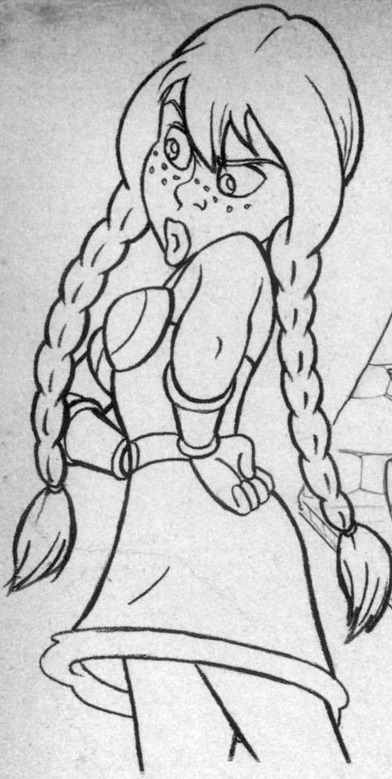

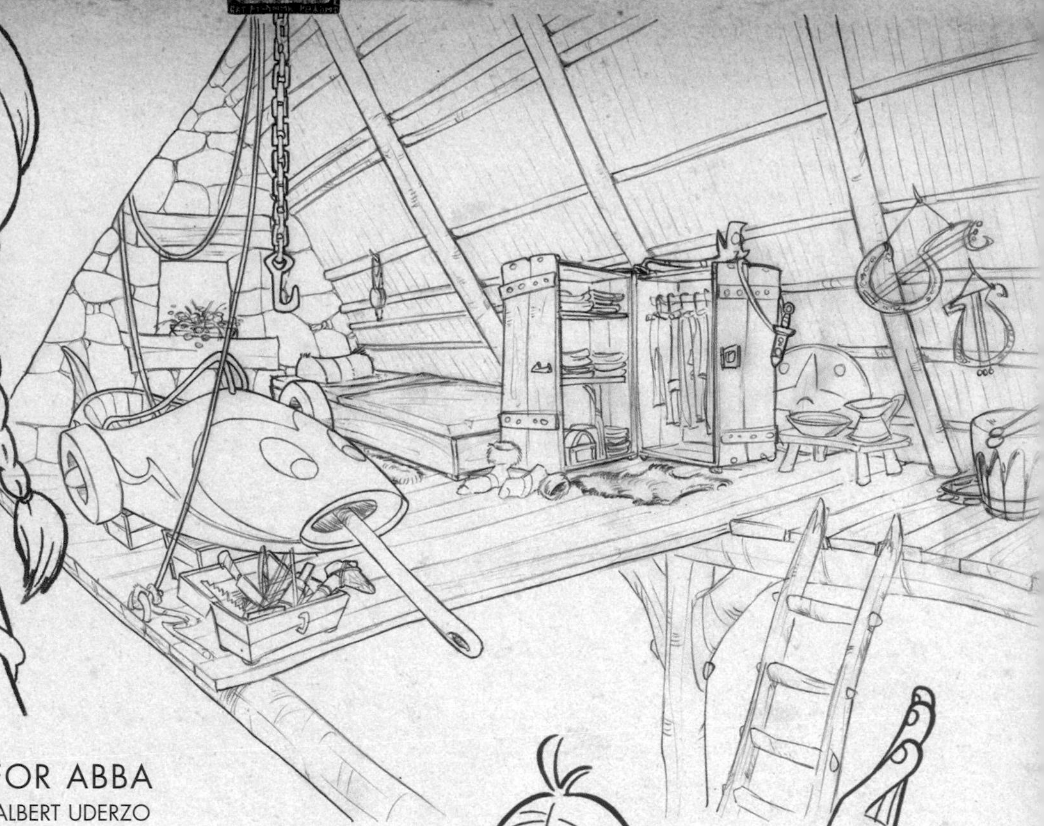

RESEARCH FOR ABBA

FOR APPROVAL BY ALBERT UDERZO

Source: M6 Studio

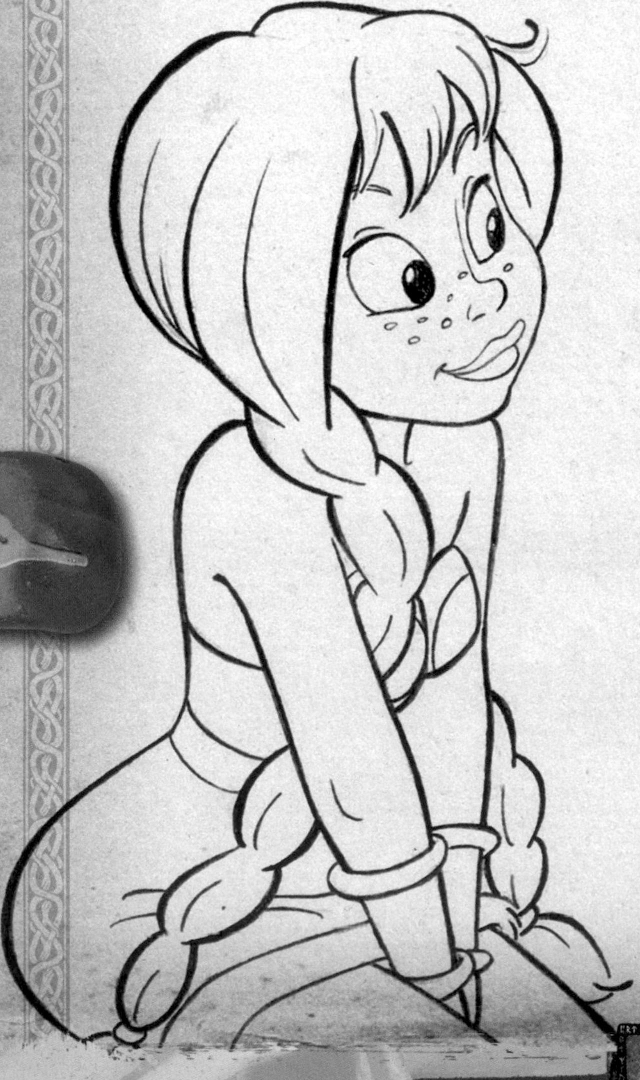

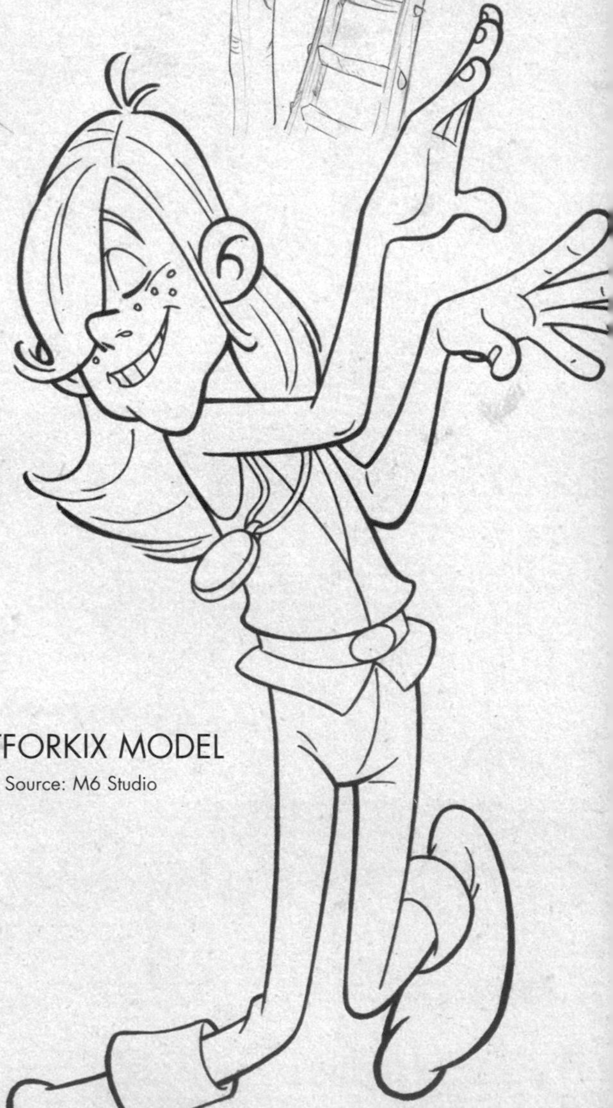

JUSTFORKIX MODEL

Source: M6 Studio

RESEARCH FOR TIMANDAHAF
FOR APPROVAL BY ALBERT UDERZO
Source: M6 Studio

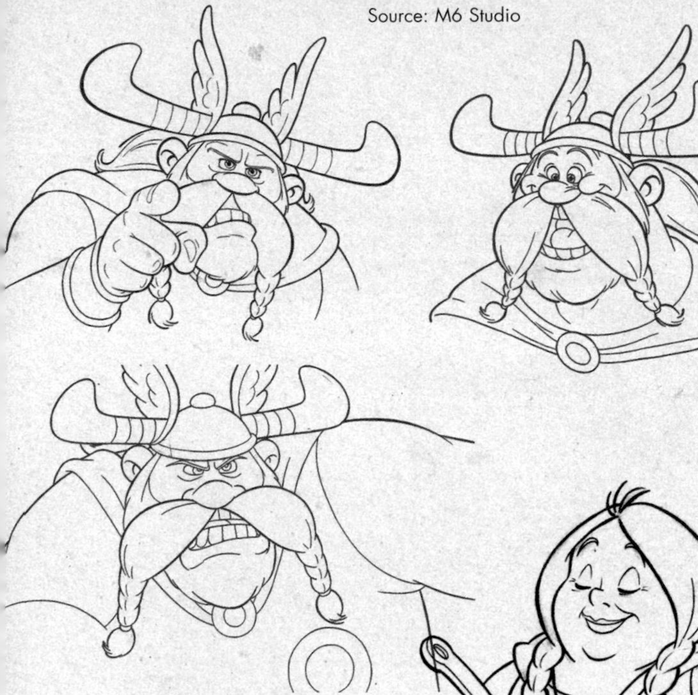

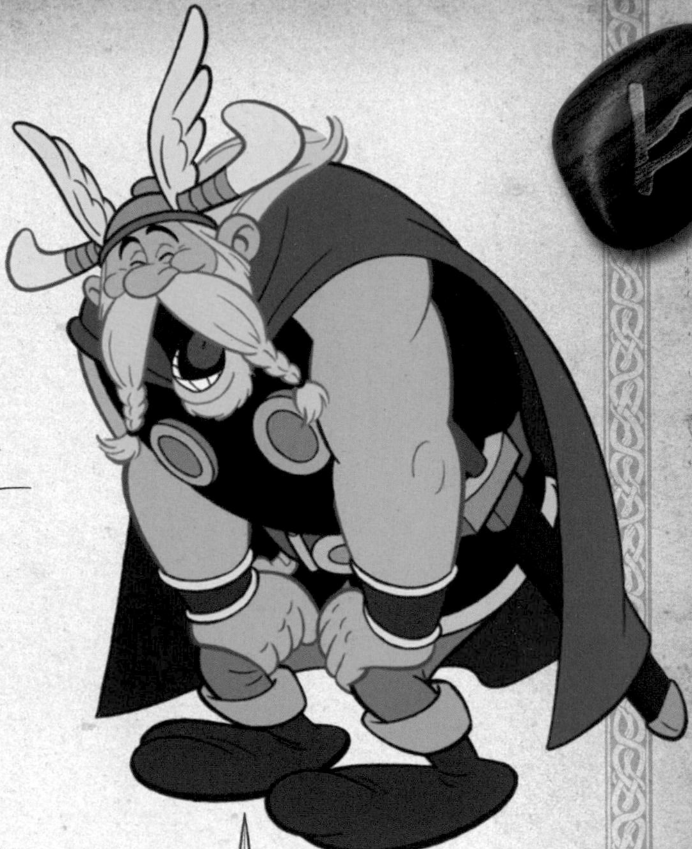

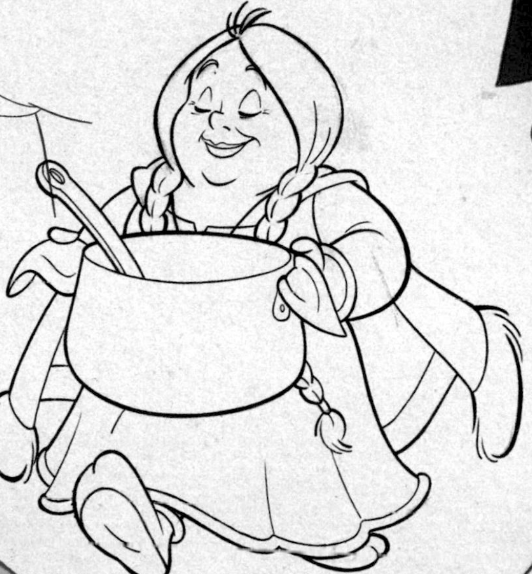

VIKEA
Source: M6 Studio

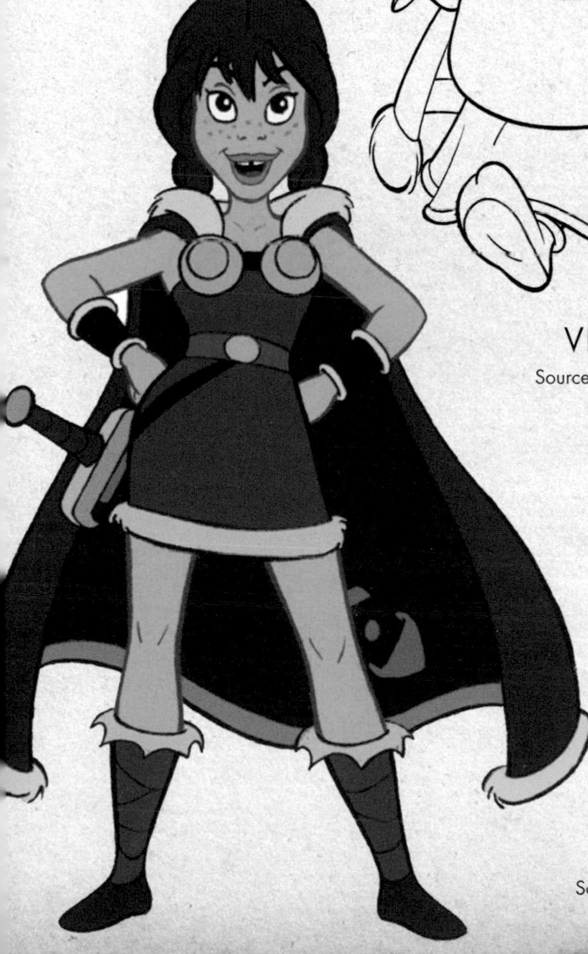

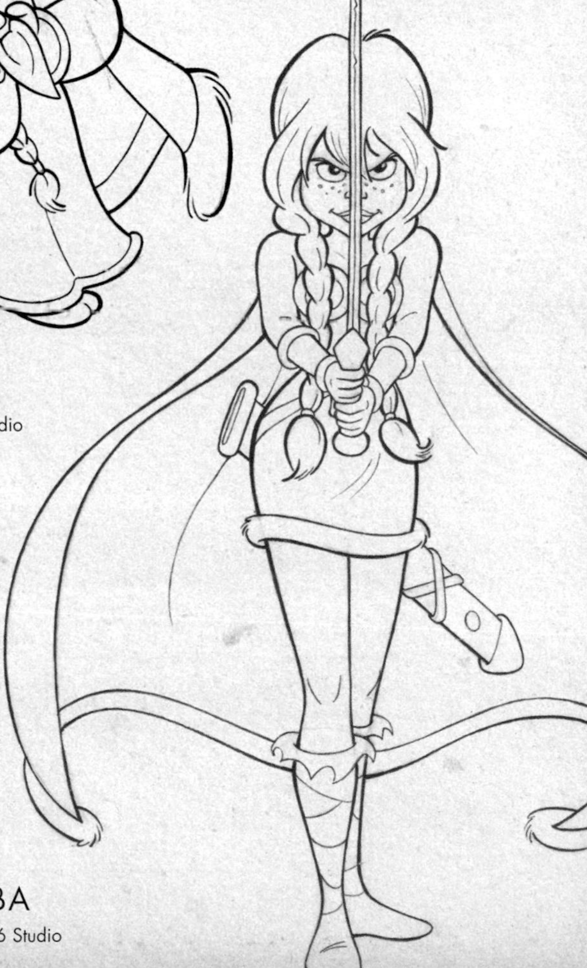

ABBA
Source: M6 Studio

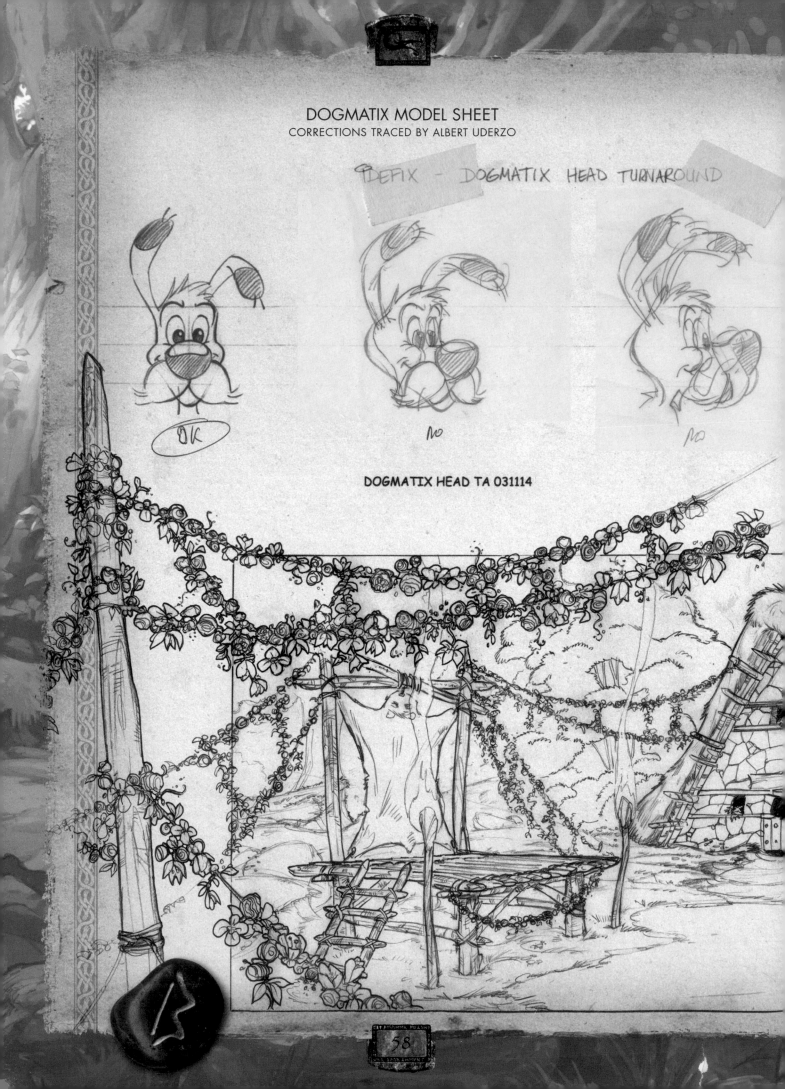

DOGMATIX MODEL SHEET

CORRECTIONS TRACED BY ALBERT UDERZO

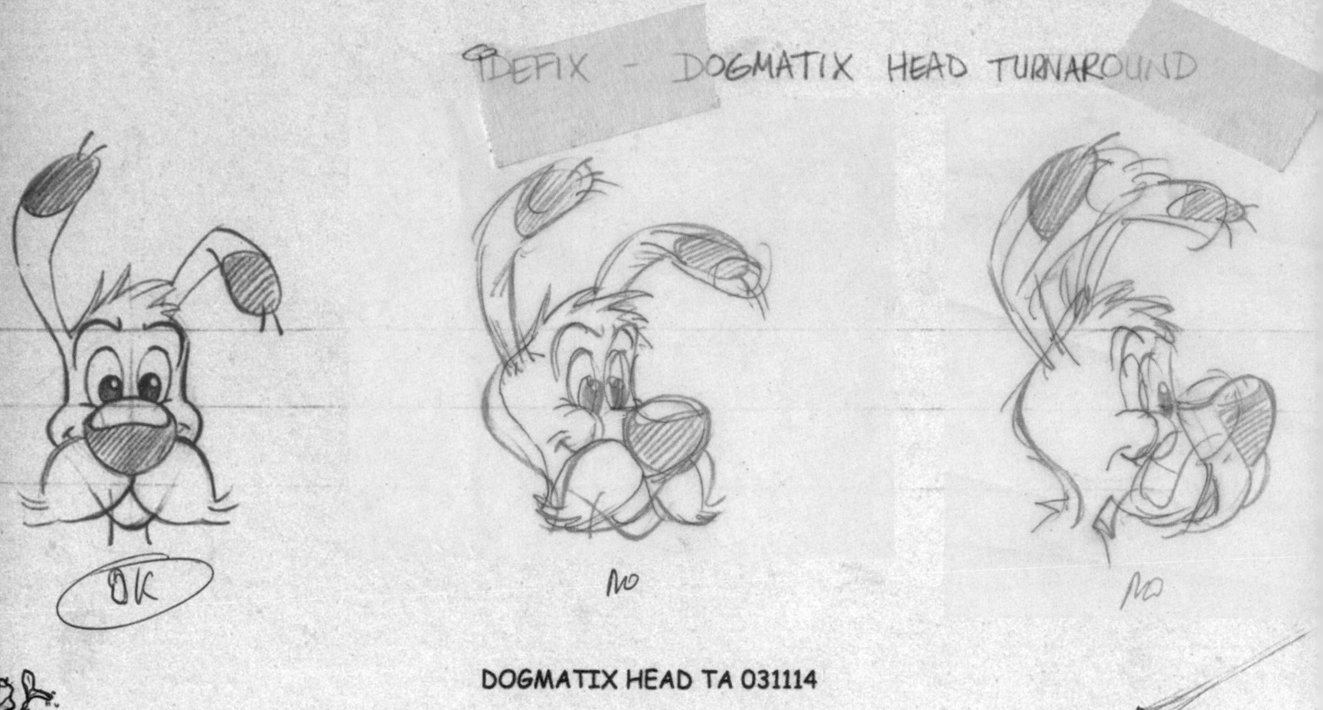
IDEFIX - DOGMATIX HEAD TURNAROUND
OK
NO
NO
DOGMATIX HEAD TA 031114

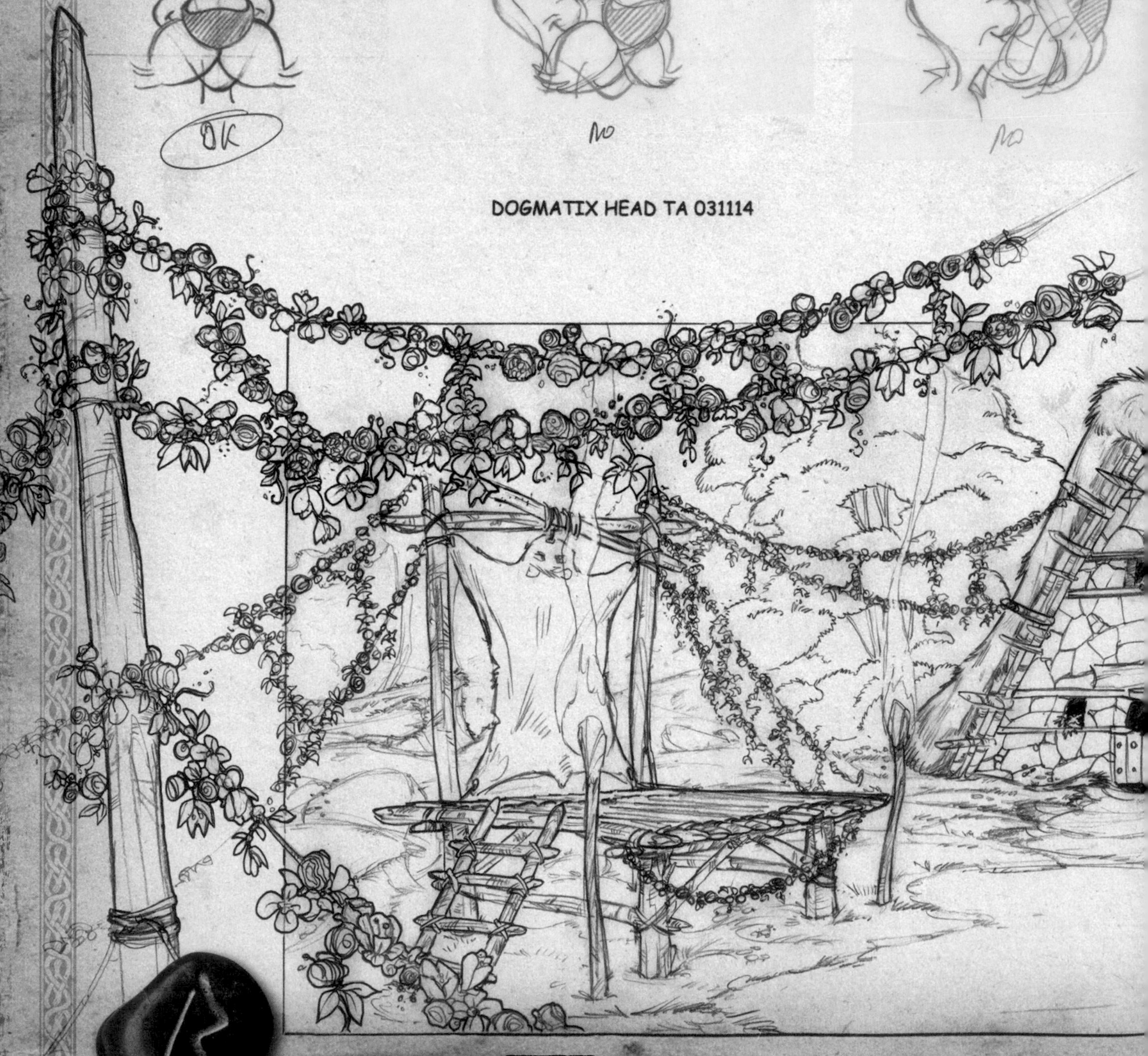

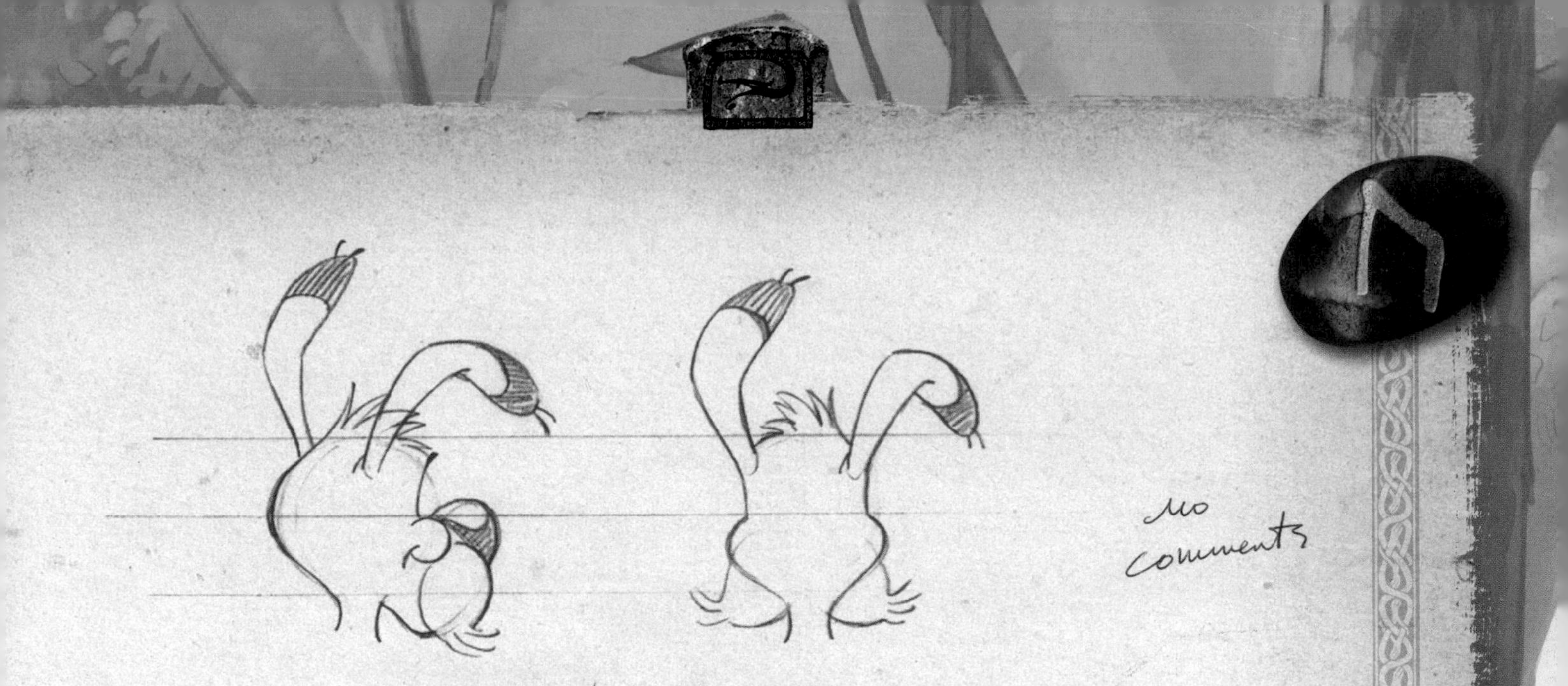

no comments

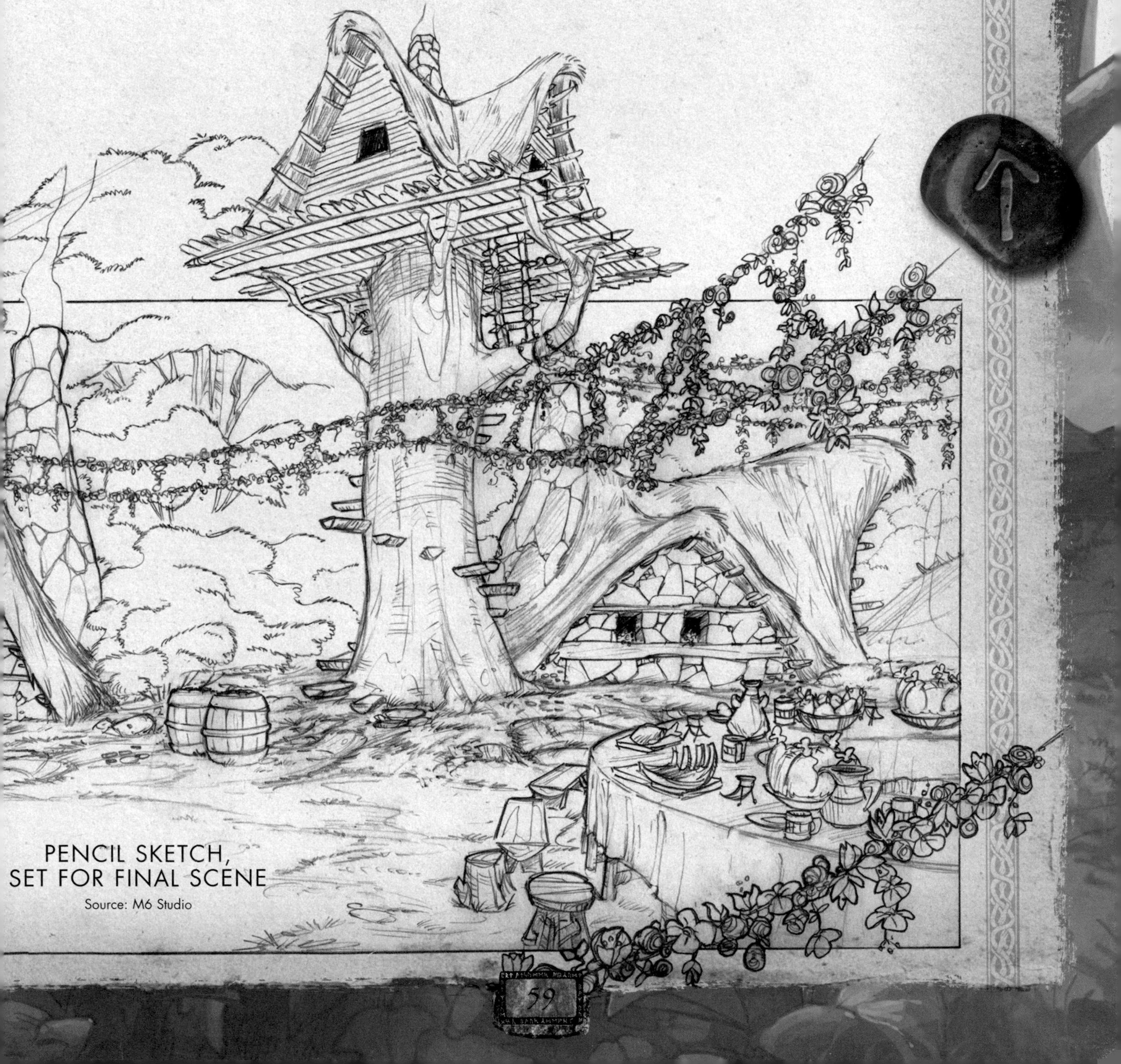

PENCIL SKETCH,
SET FOR FINAL SCENE

Source: M6 Studio

STUDY FOR SCENERY
WITH CRYPTOGRAF

Source: M6 Studio

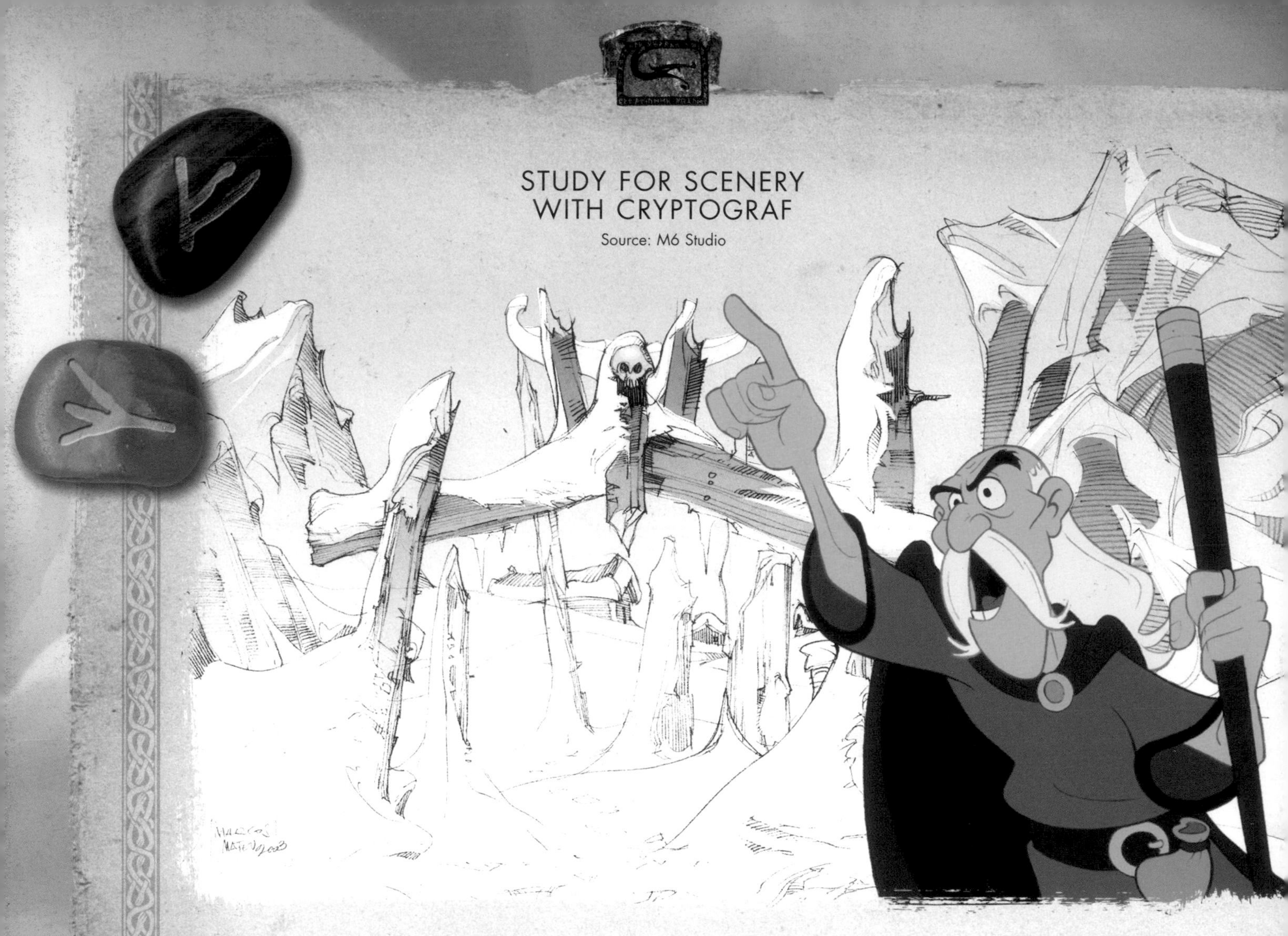

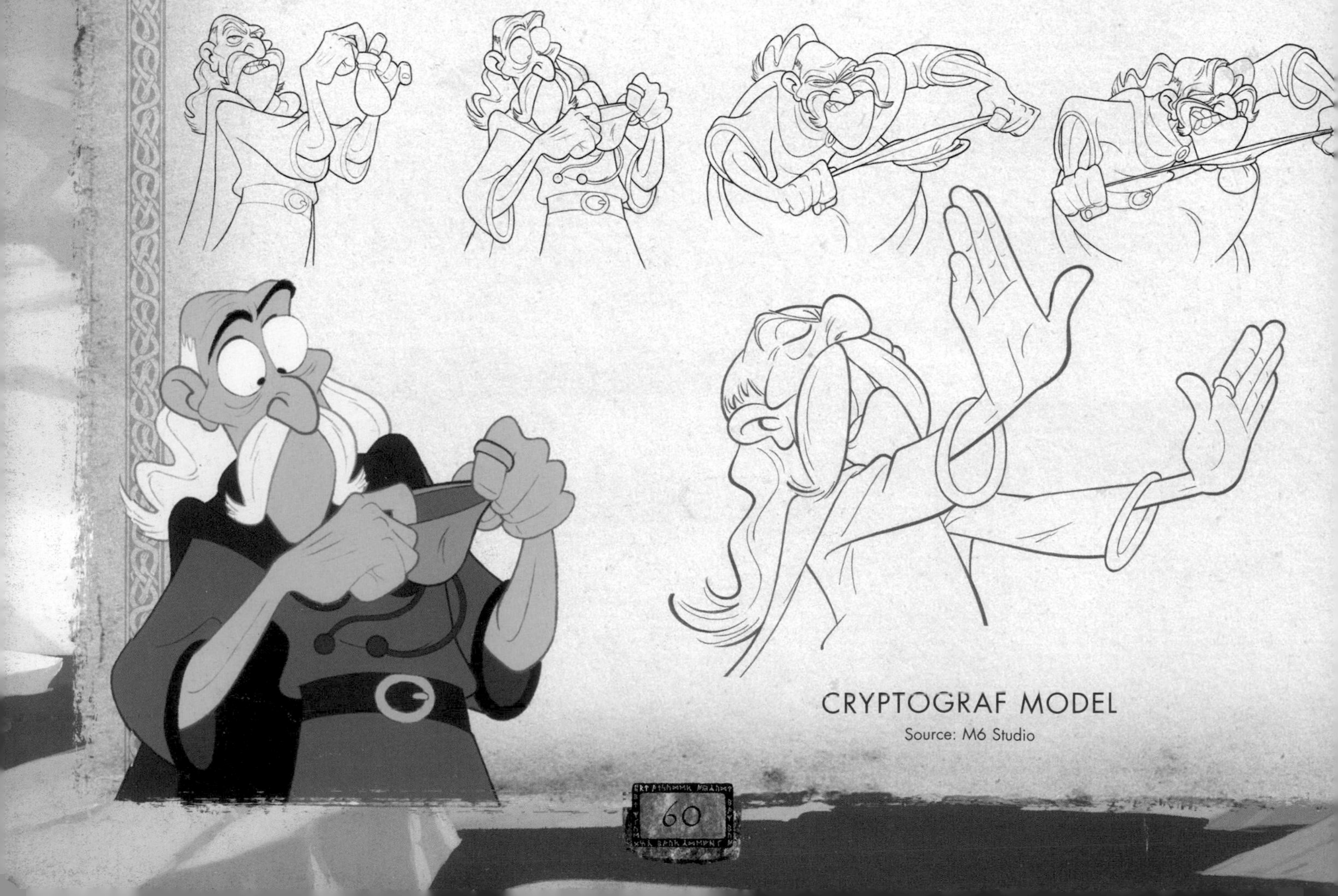

CRYPTOGRAF MODEL

Source: M6 Studio

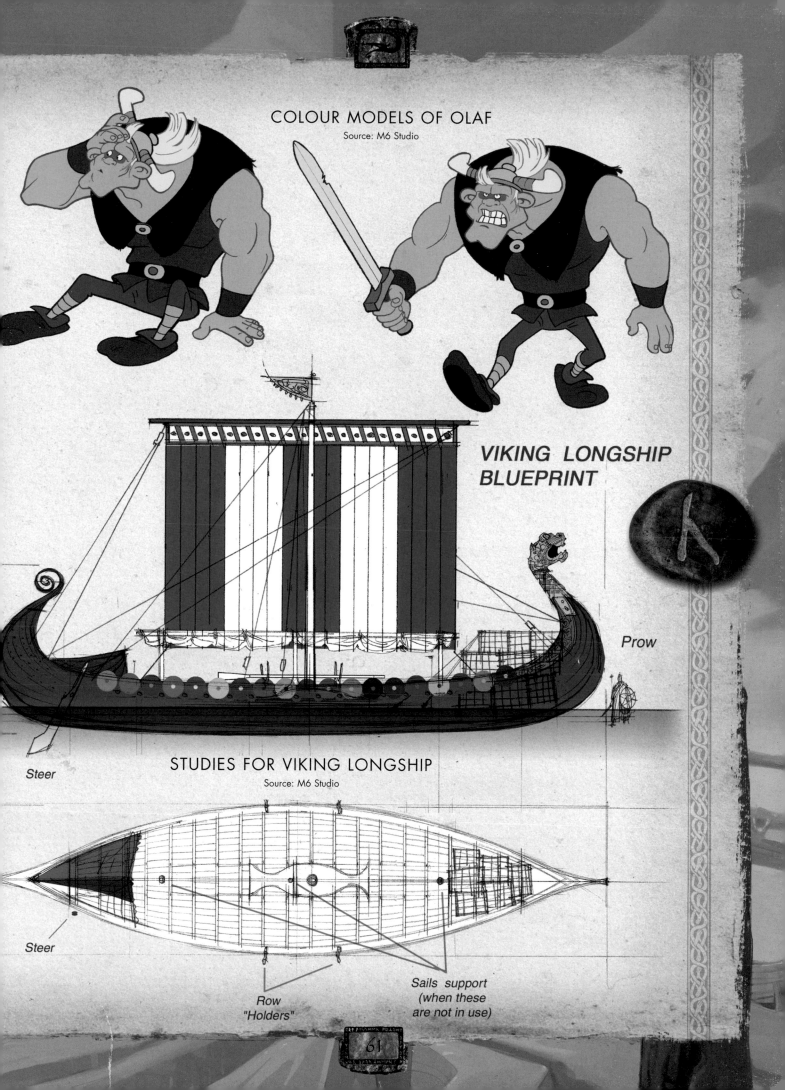

COLOUR MODELS OF OLAF

Source: M6 Studio

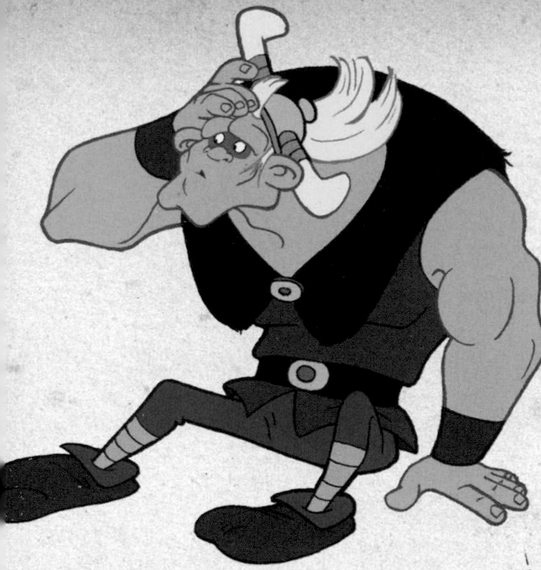

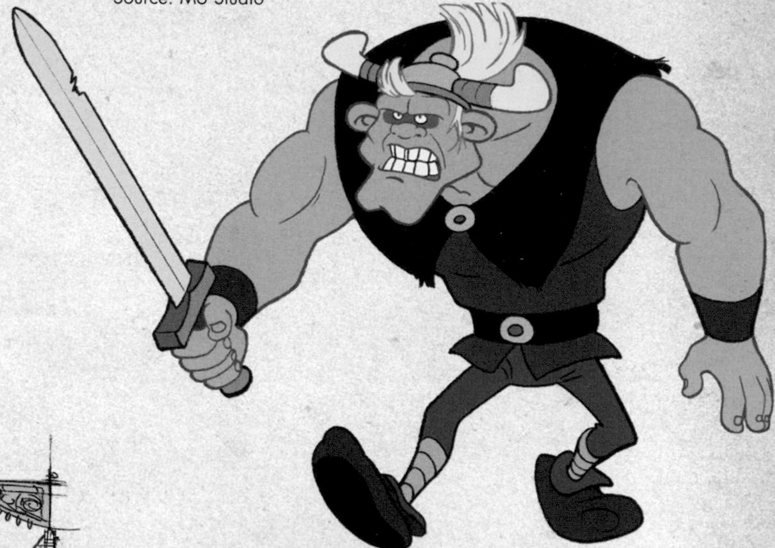

VIKING LONGSHIP BLUEPRINT

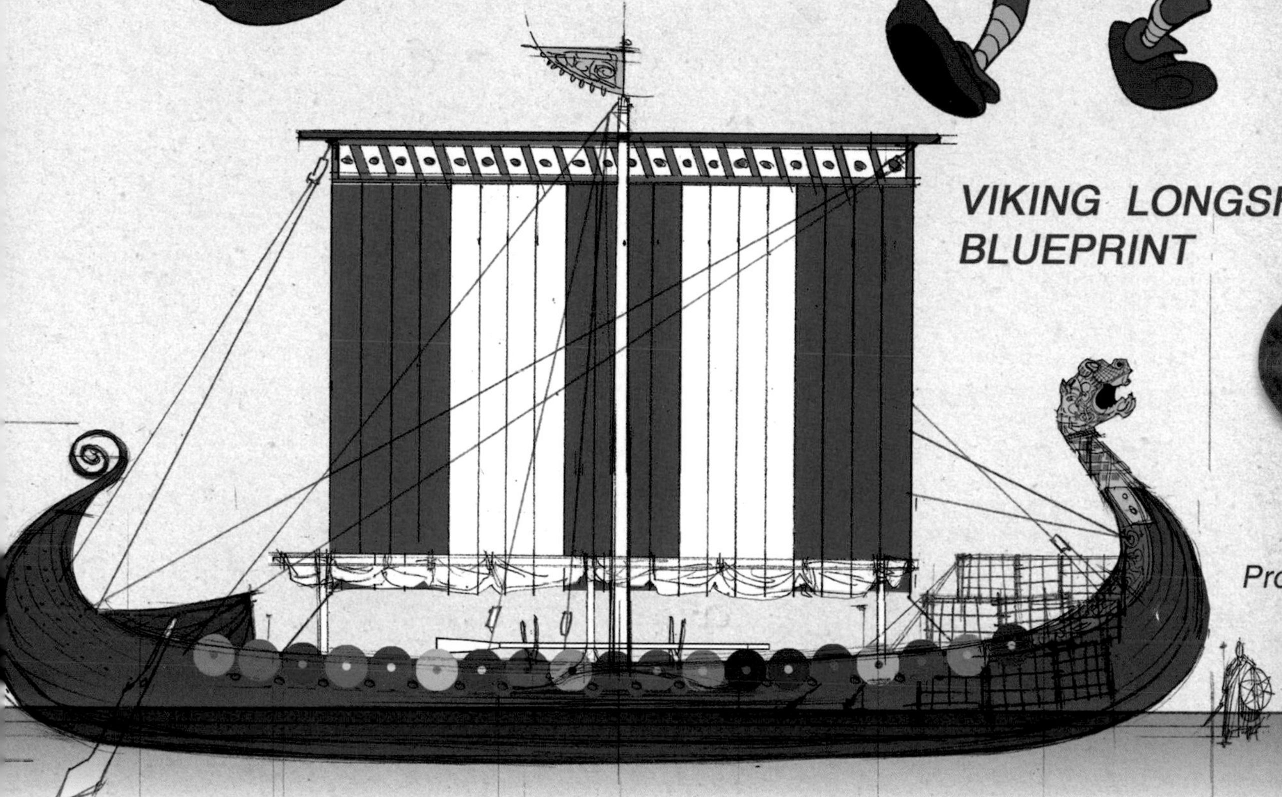
Prow
Steer

STUDIES FOR VIKING LONGSHIP

Source: M6 Studio

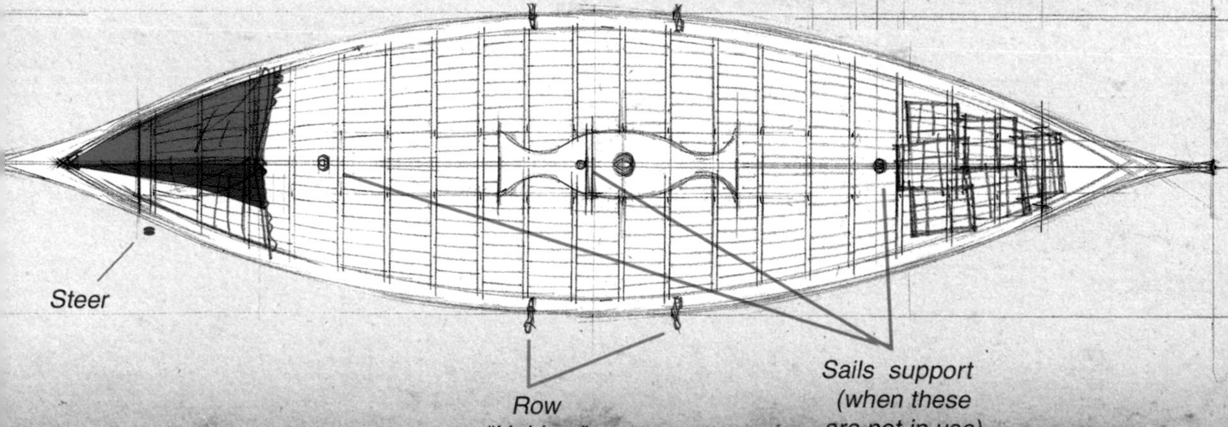
Steer
Row "Holders"
Sails support (when these are not in use)

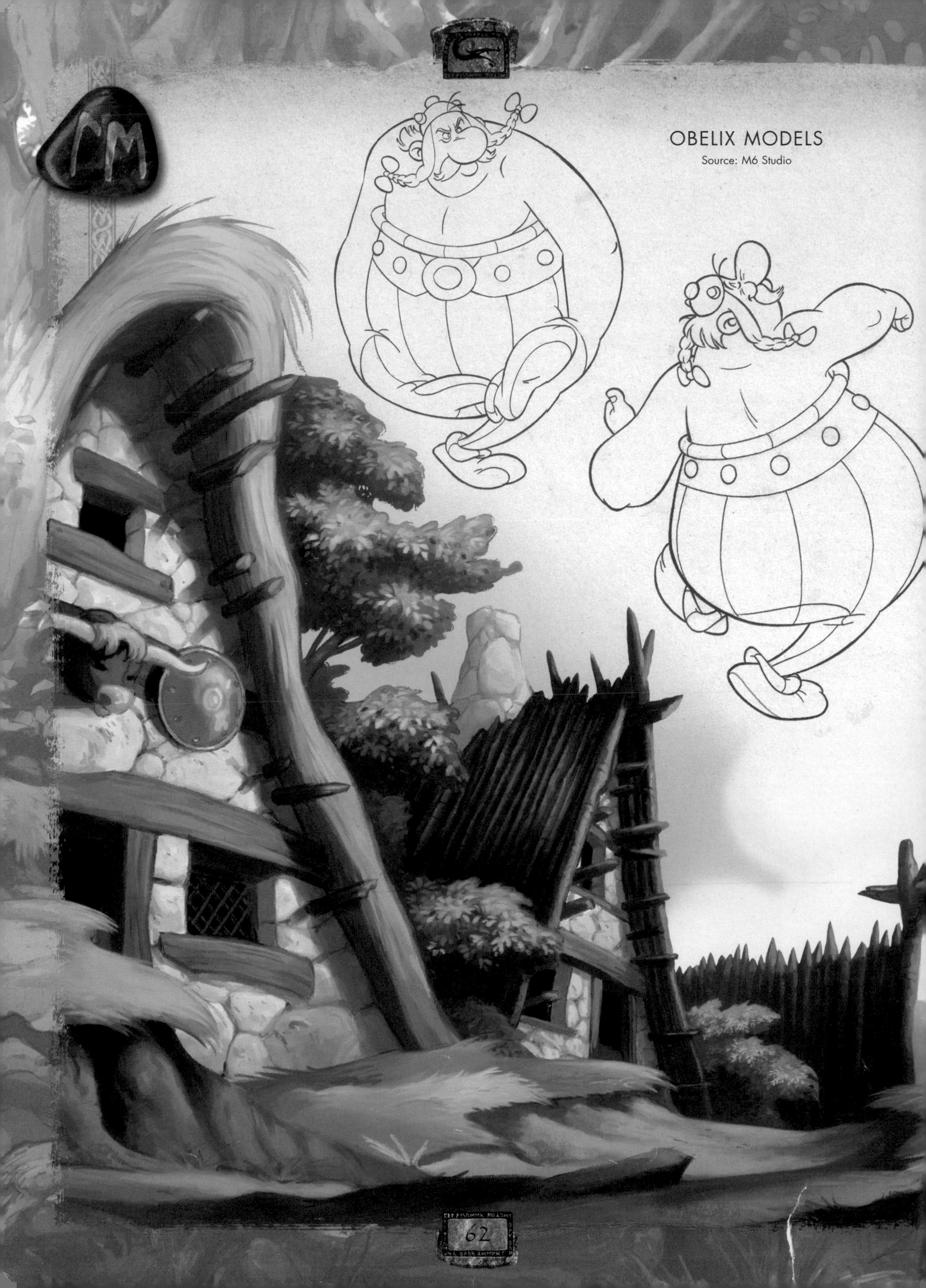

OBELIX MODELS

Source: M6 Studio

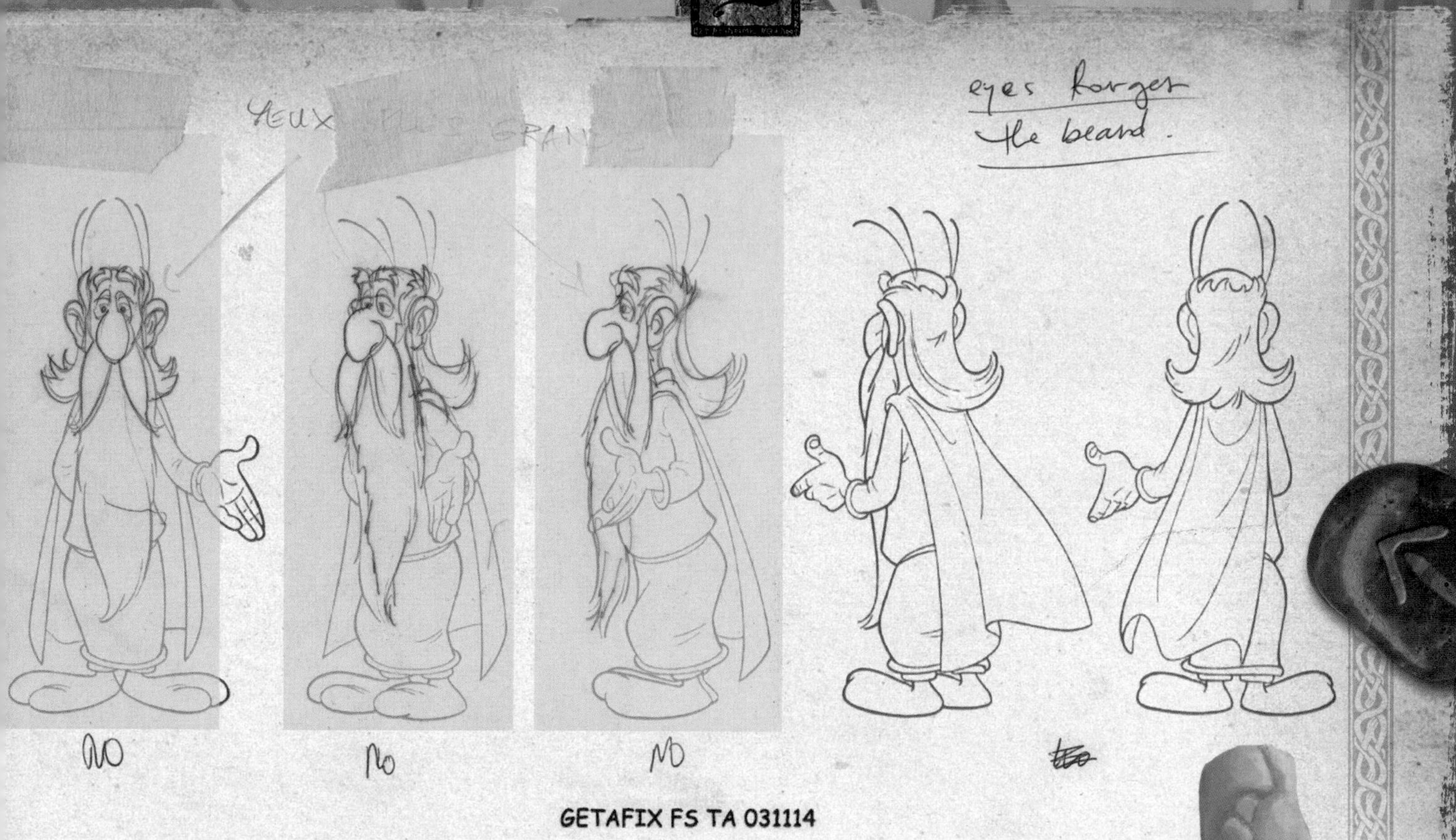
YEUX
eyes larger
the beard.
NO
No
NO
GETAFIX FS TA 031114

GETAFIX MODEL SHEET
CORRECTIONS TRACED BY ALBERT UDERZO

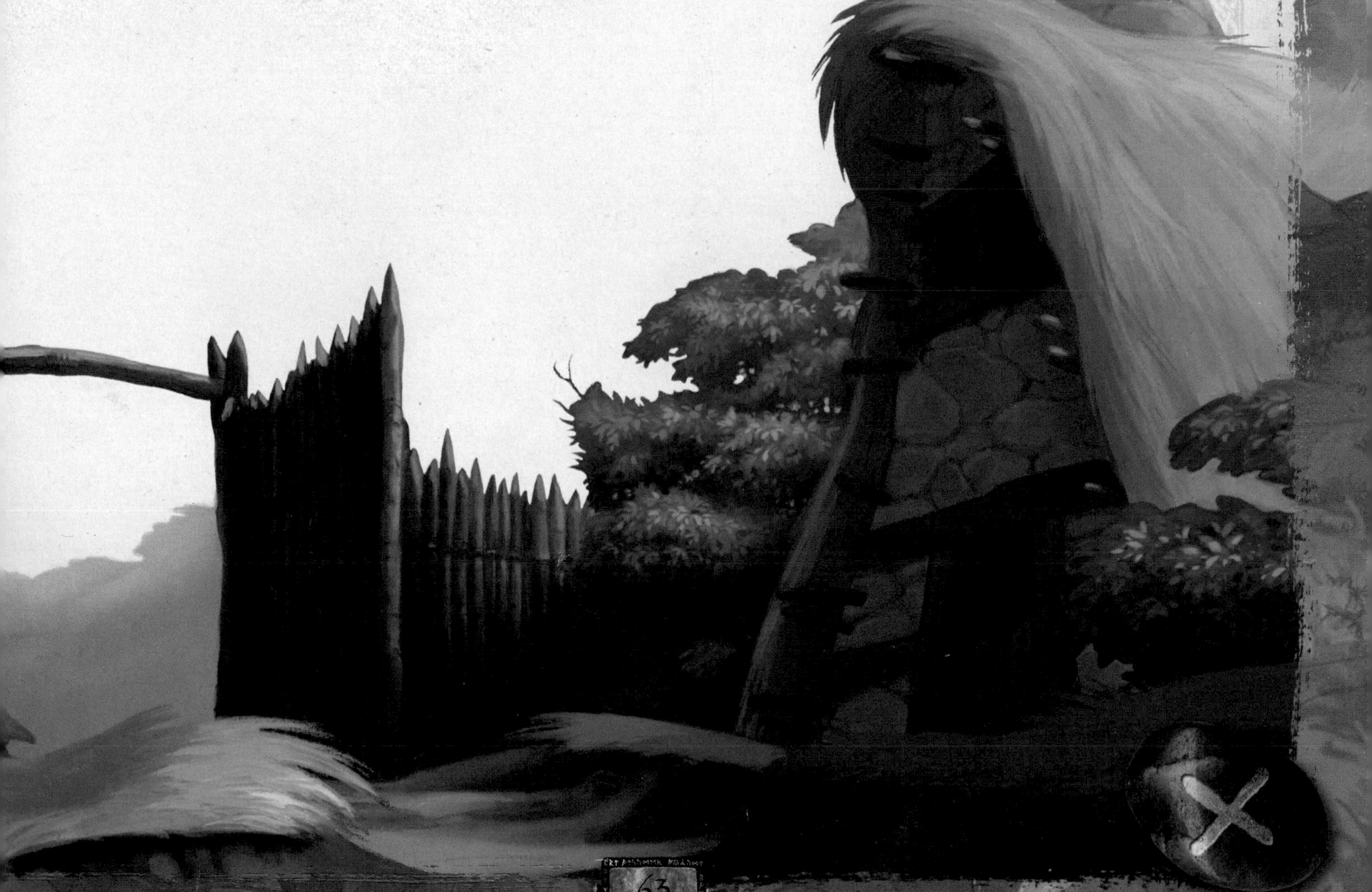

IMPEDIMENTA MODEL SHEET
CORRECTIONS TRACED BY ALBERT UDERZO

IMPEDIMENTA FS TA 031114

No comments

*general proportions
& subtle stuff*

GERIATRIX MODEL SHEET
CORRECTIONS TRACED BY ALBERT UDERZO

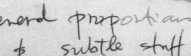

*general proportions
& subtle stuff* GERIATRIX FS TA 031031

no comments

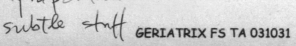

Asterix titles available now

1 Asterix the Gaul
2 Asterix and the Golden Sickle
3 Asterix and the Goths
4 Asterix the Gladiator
5 Asterix and the Banquet
6 Asterix and Cleopatra
7 Asterix and the Big Fight
8 Asterix in Britain
9 Asterix and the Normans
10 Asterix the Legionary
11 Asterix and the Chieftain's Shield
12 Asterix at the Olympic Games
13 Asterix and the Cauldron
14 Asterix in Spain
15 Asterix and the Roman Agent
16 Asterix in Switzerland
17 The Mansions of the Gods
18 Asterix and the Laurel Wreath
19 Asterix and the Soothsayer
20 Asterix in Corsica
21 Asterix and Caesar's Gift
22 Asterix and the Great Crossing
23 Obelix and Co.
24 Asterix in Belgium
25 Asterix and the Great Divide
26 Asterix and the Black Gold
27 Asterix and Son
28 Asterix and the Magic Carpet
29 Asterix and the Secret Weapon
30 Asterix and Obelix All at Sea
31 Asterix and the Actress
32 Asterix and the Class Act
33 Asterix and the Falling Sky
34 Asterix and Obelix's Birthday – the Golden Book
35 Asterix and the Picts
36 Asterix and the Missing Scroll

Where's Asterix?
Where's Dogmatix?
Asterix and the Vikings
Asterix at the Olympic Games (film tie-in)
How Obelix Fell into the Magic Potion
Asterix Omnibus 1 (Books 1-3)
Asterix Omnibus 2 (Books 4-6)
Asterix Omnibus 3 (Books 7-9)
Asterix Omnibus 4 (Books 10-12)
Asterix Omnibus 5 (Books 13-15)
Asterix Omnibus 6 (Books 16-18)
Asterix Omnibus 7 (Books 19-21)
Asterix Omnibus 8 (Books 22-24)
Asterix Omnibus 9 (Books 25-27)
Asterix Omnibus 10 (Books 28-30)
Asterix Omnibus 11 (Books 31-33)

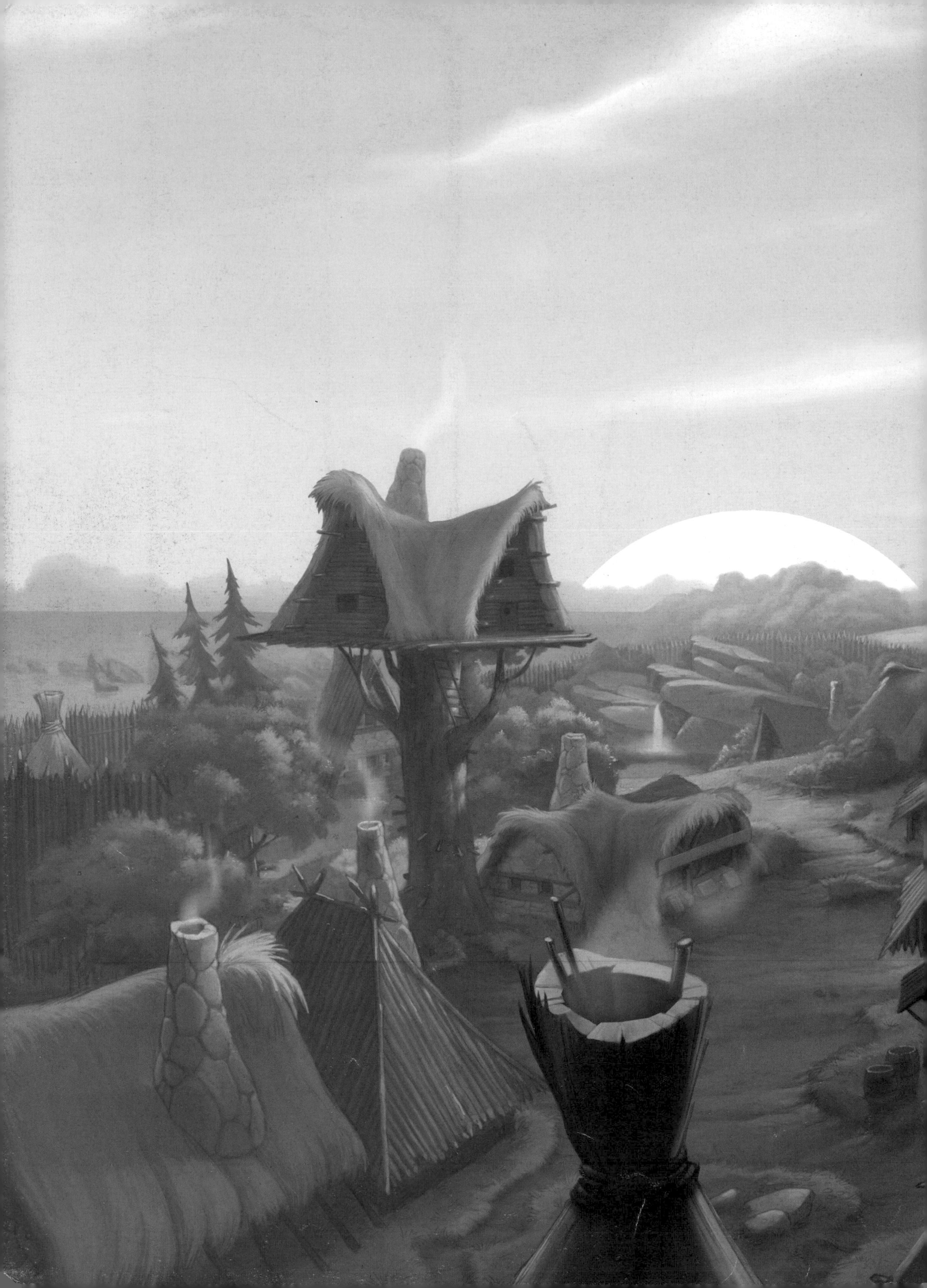

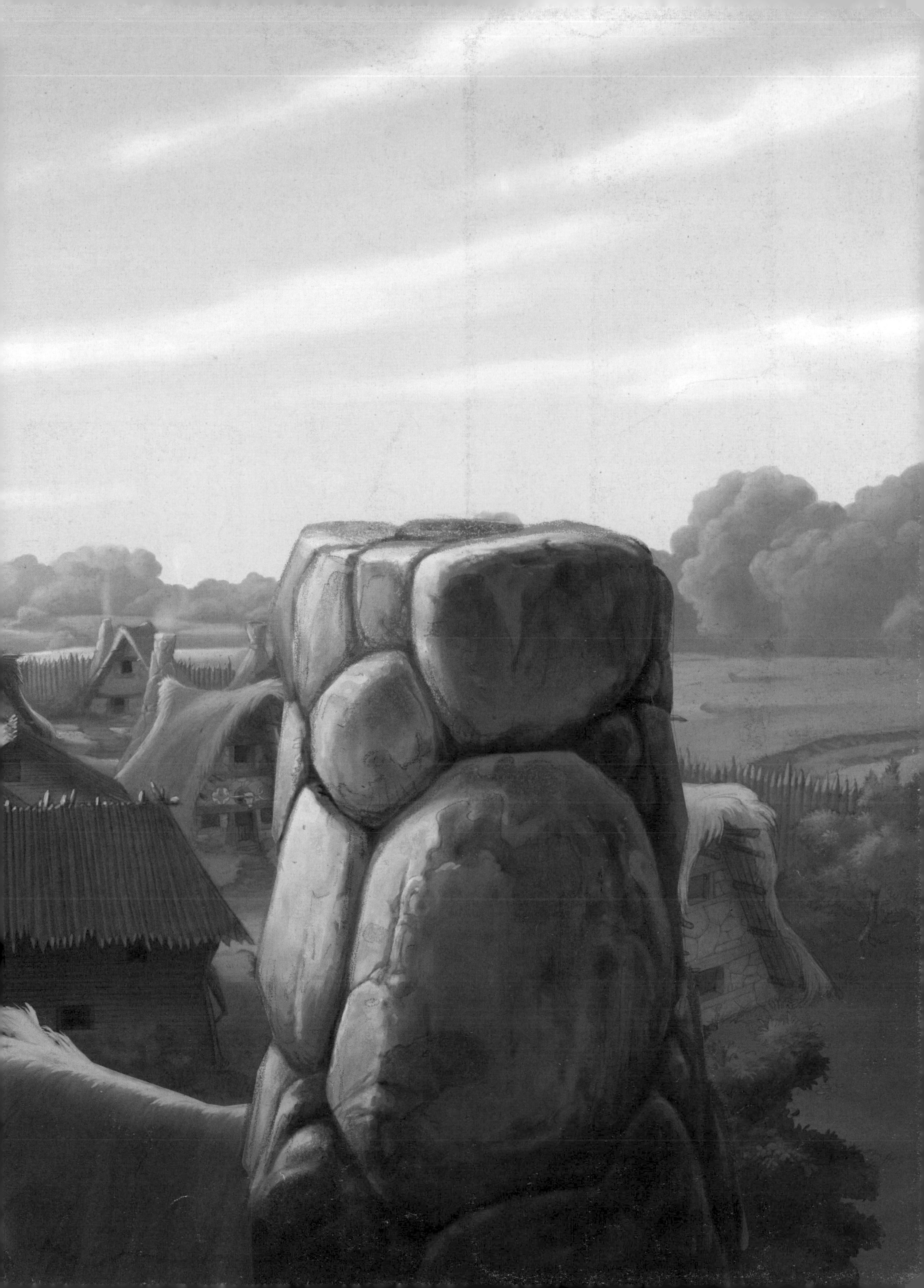